She was in trouble

Kylie took another peek through the peephole. Yep, Drew was looking as hot as ever. She opened the door and stood aside for him to enter, forgetting for a moment that she was clad in only a towel.

"Hey, I like what you're wearing tonight," he said.

"Is it too much for dinner, do you think?"

She could feel the heat in his eyes, warming her wherever he looked.

Definitely she was in big, big trouble.

"There's just one thing," Drew said, reaching out. "It looks like it would fall off easily."

She didn't try to stop him as he gave the towel a gentle tug. It fell to the floor and she stood there naked, a raging heat starting low in her belly.

"See what I mean?" He traced his finger along one breast. "Uh-oh, you're getting cold," he murmured. "Maybe I'd better help warm you up...."

Blaze™

Dear Reader,

Throughout my life I've been drawn again and again
to the romance of the ocean. There's something
about its rhythms and depths I find irresistible. So
I really enjoyed creating Drew and Kylie, who share
my love of the sea. And while the icy Pacific of the
California coast is the ocean I experience in my daily
life, I think you can guess by the content of this book
that I simply adore the warmer water of the tropics.
What better setting for a steamy romance?

I love to hear from readers, so write and let me
know what you think of *Seducing a S.E.A.L.*
You can reach me through my Web site,
www.jamiesobrato.com, or via e-mail at
jamiesobrato@yahoo.com. I'm also on Myspace
at www.myspace.com/jamiesobrato.

Sincerely,

Jamie Sobrato

SEDUCING
A S.E.A.L.
Jamie Sobrato

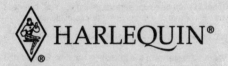

HARLEQUIN®

TORONTO • NEW YORK • LONDON
AMSTERDAM • PARIS • SYDNEY • HAMBURG
STOCKHOLM • ATHENS • TOKYO • MILAN • MADRID
PRAGUE • WARSAW • BUDAPEST • AUCKLAND

ISBN-13: 978-0-373-79424-9
ISBN-10:   0-373-79424-X

SEDUCING A S.E.A.L.

Printed in U.S.A.

ABOUT THE AUTHOR

Jamie Sobrato's first aspiration as a young child was to join the navy, mostly because she wanted to explore the world by sea and she thought the uniforms were cute. Lucky for our national defense, she went on to use her primary talents—daydreaming and procrastinating—to become a writer instead. Jamie lives in Northern California with her two young children and two house rabbits who think they rule the world. *Seducing a S.E.A.L.* is her fifteenth novel for Harlequin Books. No S.E.A.L.s were harmed during the writing of this book.

To my dad, Russ Bush, a true survivor.
Thank you for all your love and support.

Prologue

KYLIE HEARD the gunshots first, then the screams.

Shots? This was not a war zone. She was a Naval officer, yes. But she was in San Diego, not Baghdad.

Her fingers halted on the computer keyboard, and as adrenaline kicked in, she pushed back from her desk and sent her wheeled chair careening across the room as she shot out of it toward the door. Her instincts had her taking inventory of the soldiers and civilians at work, then Ensign MacLeod raced past her door, calling out for everyone to take cover.

But this was her office, her people. And as lieutenant commander, it was her job to defuse the situation. She ran toward the sounds of chaos coming from the reception area at the front of the building. A man yelling, another gunshot, more screams.

She couldn't let anyone get hurt on her watch.

Her hand slipped into her pocket and pulled out a cell phone, dialed the military police. As she entered another hallway, she was met by a wall of chest. Hands grabbing her and pulling her into an office. She struggled, then realized it was Ensign MacLeod who held her.

"Stay here," he ordered, his voice low. "There's a gunman in the building."

Kylie looked at him, confused. How could this be happening? Despite the evidence, her mind struggled to grasp the situation. A voice on her cell phone focused her thoughts. "A gunman," she repeated into the phone. "I'm in Building 2024. There's a gunman. He's already fired several rounds. People may be hurt. We need help *right now!*"

She didn't hear what the dispatcher said next. All she heard was the round of gunfire, another scream and a man's voice demanding, "Where's Thomas?"

That was her.

She had to get out there. She had to face that man and figure out how to disarm him before anyone else got in his way.

But Ensign MacLeod was tugging her across the room, away from the door he'd just closed behind them and cursed for its lack of a lock. "Out the window," he said.

"No. He wants me. I have to confront him so no one else gets hurt."

Before either of them could argue further, the door swung open, and they faced a man pointing an assault rifle at them.

Not just a nameless stranger, though. He was a seaman who'd been under Kylie's command until a week ago, when she'd filed dishonorable discharge papers on him for his having raped a fellow sailor.

"Seaman Caldwell," she forced herself to say calmly. "Please put down the gun and tell me why you're here."

"Shut up, bitch. Both of you on the floor, now!"

1

HE WAS MUCH TOO YOUNG for her. Eight years too young, according to his military record.

Off-limits for her.

And there was the fact that he worked for her. This was the U.S. Navy, not a daytime soap opera, so rank was huge.

Definitely off-limits.

And she, a Naval Academy grad, knew better than to entertain such thoughts as her and him getting way cozier than regulations allowed. Especially given their current circumstances. The tragedy, the trauma, the grief she was supposed to be focusing on.

Absolutely forbidden.

But grief, so foreign to her relatively calm life, did strange things to her. Such as lust after inappropriate men.

It wouldn't have been quite so disturbing if she'd kept the fantasies on a purely sexual level. That would have been normal given that she was a woman with a healthy libido and he was nearly six feet of golden-haired, bronze-skinned, blue-eyed perfection.

But no, when she let her mind wander into forbidden territory, the images were often cozy, domestic vignettes of her and Ensign Drew MacLeod frolicking on a beach or playing around while cooking, acting like a couple in a clichéd romantic comedy. Her fantasies were dangerously close to the kind that meant she was falling into something more than lust with the oblivious younger man. Because he'd never shown a sign of being aware of her as anything more than his boss. He'd always behaved respectfully and properly. As had she…in real life, if not in her mind.

Lieutenant Commander Kylie Thomas tore her gaze from the man she'd been daydreaming about regularly for the past year since he'd been transferred to her office—and dreaming of almost nonstop since their ordeal a week ago—then forced herself to focus on the therapist, Judith, who was leading their group counseling session.

"I'd like all of you to close your eyes and visualize yourselves in a peaceful place," Judith said. "Perhaps in a field of flowers, or on a mountaintop or in a comfortable chair by a fireplace. Find an image that soothes you, and go there…. Breathe deeply, in and out…in and out…"

Kylie had never been in therapy before, and already, five minutes into her first session, she hated it. How the hell would flowers or fireplaces help her accept her failure to perform in a critical moment? It couldn't. Nothing could except working her ass off to regain the confidence of her superiors.

Stifling a sigh, she closed her eyes. The first image that came to mind was that old bumper sticker that read Visualize Whirled Peas.

A giggle erupted from her throat, and she fought to prevent any more from escaping. She had a problem with inappropriate laughter, as well as inappropriate fantasies, apparently. Inexplicable laughter had bubbled out on several inopportune occasions since the shooting.

The other three people in the session glanced at her, perplexed, and she covered her mouth.

"I'm sorry," she whispered when she'd regained control. "I've been doing that a lot lately. The laughing, I mean. I was just thinking of that bumper sticker Visualize Whirled Peas. I guess when you said *visualize* it triggered the memory and, you know, peas are so far from mountains I just found it funny."

Oh dear God, she was rambling now, making no sense.

Judith nodded and saved Kylie from herself as everyone else in the group stared at her as if she'd lost her mind.

"Stress and grief can evoke highly emotional responses that may not seem appropriate to us. It's often our body's way of releasing the stress in a way that feels most natural, safe. Laughter, as a physical response, really isn't so different from crying."

Judith made a point of looking at each person in the circle of chairs, bestowing her gaze on them in soothing little doses—first Ensign MacLeod, then Chief Jones, then Lieutenant Humphrey, then Kylie. This all seemed so contrived to Kylie, so let's-hold-hands-and-sing-"Kumbaya." This touchy-feely stuff was so unlike the rule and regulation-loving Navy that it surprised her the survivors of the shooting had been ordered into this mandatory counseling. Leave it to the military to micromanage the grief process.

Still, mandatory counseling was at least more appropriate than nursing a crush on her subordinate, the one who'd been involved in the most horrific event of her life.

Tomorrow, she'd be here again for an individual therapy session, and she wondered if she'd have the courage to admit her crush. Would she be able to confess she'd been unable to stop imagining them as a couple after those moments alone in that office. There probably was some psychological explanation for the fantasies, but she wasn't sure she wanted to hear it.

In spite of the counselor's soothing words, everyone seemed to be a little ill at ease after Kylie's giggling outburst, so Judith guided them toward talking.

"Has anyone else experienced what seems like an inappropriate response to the trauma you've experienced?" She looked slowly around the room again, waiting for responses.

Silence.

Chief Jones cleared his throat, but said nothing.

Okay, so Kylie was the only nut job in the room.

Or perhaps she was the one with the most incentive to avoid facing her grief, since she'd been responsible for those who'd died. Four of her subordinates. One civilian and three sailors. She'd stood by and watched them die. She'd been powerless to stop it.

Four funerals attended. Six children now grieving the loss of parents. Countless people's lives affected.

When she wasn't engaging in shameful escapist fantasies or laughing at inopportune moments, she was seized by a pain so intense it was beyond her ability to cope.

"Let's start by going around the room and taking turns talking for a few minutes about whatever is on your mind. If you've got a question or issue you'd like to ask the group, you may do that, as well."

Everyone murmured assent.

"We'll start with you, Drew. What's been going on with you since the shooting?"

Kylie watched as he shifted in his hard, green plastic seat. He glanced down at his lap and smoothed his faded jeans along his thighs.

"I've been having trouble sleeping," he said. "I close my eyes and see the shooting happening all over again. I keep thinking how I could have done things differently…and maybe saved someone."

"Those are common symptoms of post-traumatic stress disorder," Judith said. "It sounds as if you felt powerless during the attack."

Drew's expression turned dark. "Yeah, I guess I did."

"Hey, man, if it wasn't for you, we might have all been dead," Lieutenant Humphrey said.

Drew shook his head.

"Hard as it may be to do, it's important to hang on to positive thoughts during this time." Judith spoke directly to Drew before including the other group members. "When you feel your thoughts going in a negative direction, when you begin to berate yourself for what you could have done differently—try to think of something you have control over or something you did that you can feel proud of instead."

Everyone was silent, and Kylie imagined they were

all resisting the encouragement to feel proud about anything in the face of their coworkers' deaths. Clearly Judith had not been there.

Kylie squeezed her eyes shut tight and bit her lip, another wave of giggles threatening to burst out of her at how ridiculous the therapist sounded. Feel proud? Yeah, right. But even mentally mocking Judith didn't ease Kylie's urge to laugh. If she didn't laugh, she'd cry. And if she started crying, she was afraid she wouldn't be able to stop.

And female Navy lieutenant commanders did not ever, ever, ever cry in front of their people.

"Kylie, would you like to take a turn now at talking a bit about what you've been going through?"

Kylie's gaze connected with Judith's, and the sudden pressure to participate without unleashing her inner grief and while showing the leadership and control demanded of her rank effectively eliminated her laughter.

"Okay," Kylie said. "I guess I've been having the opposite problem of Ensign MacLeod. I avoid thinking about what happened, and I find myself daydreaming too much. Thinking about things I shouldn't, just to keep from having to dwell on the shooting."

"What sorts of things do you daydream about?"

Kylie felt herself blush. She hadn't intended to confess to the fantasizing right here and now, but the words had escaped anyway.

"You know, it's sort of like how you were telling us to imagine ourselves in a calm, peaceful place. Like in a field of flowers or something. I keep imagining myself content and living out normal domestic scenes.

Only happier. Like I'm starring in a movie about my life."

"And does this bother you?"

"Well, yeah. I should be thinking about what happened. They were good people and they deserve my attention…my respect…all the time. It was so tragic, it feels wrong to think about anything else. And that's all I do—think about other stuff."

"It's natural to avoid thinking about things our emotional self has trouble processing."

Kylie avoided Judith's gaze. "Yeah, I guess so."

"Isn't it interesting that you're naturally doing what I've advised Drew to do—to think positive thoughts? It's a self-preservation mechanism."

"But isn't it just avoidance?"

"I suggest you allow yourself to think about what happened only as much as you feel you can handle at any given time. Perhaps in individual therapy sessions with me to support you and no audience will be a safer environment for you."

Kylie nodded, though her insides seized at the thought of breaking down and letting out what was building up inside her. Shame, terror, grief—all of it too big and loud to let out in front of anyone.

Four funerals and one memorial service attended, her eyes had remained dry through each one. She was a coward in ways she'd never imagined, because she couldn't face the demons inside herself any more than she could face the challenge of the demons walking around in the world.

Lieutenant Humphrey was talking now, and she owed him her focus. He was talking about things he'd seen, feelings he'd had that day…. He could have been talking for her, their experiences had been so similar.

But her mind refused to cooperate. She pretended to pay attention, while in her mind, the movie began to play again.

A sunny beach. A warm, tropical breeze. Skin bare in the sun. Flesh cooled while sinking into the water, waves lapping at her belly…Drew's hands on her, teasing her, pleasing her, arousing her, pulling her farther toward the surf. His mouth, gentle and demanding at the same time, kissing her, then finding all the places that ached for his attention….

2

"C'MON MAN, KEEP GOING. Don't be a quitter."

The cruel hand pressing down against the middle of Drew's back disappeared, and his muscles screamed for him to stop. Pain gave way to intense burning, and sweat dripped from his brow onto the wood floor beneath him.

Ninety-eight, ninety-nine, one hundred. After the last push-up, he collapsed onto his stomach, his arms jelly after having done all but the last five reps with his buddy Justin pressing extra weight on his back.

Now one hundred sit-ups and he'd be done with his warm-up and ready for his ten mile run. Channeling his energy into training for the S.E.A.L. test was all that kept him sane lately.

"On your back," Justin ordered, and Drew forced himself over and into the sit-up position. Justin planted himself on Drew's feet to hold them still.

"When you make the S.E.A.L. team, I expect you to repay me with many beers, man."

Drew ignored him and began the exercise while Justin counted reps. Justin was a S.E.A.L., and he'd been acting as Drew's coach for the past three months. And since the shooting, he'd been at Drew's side every day, urging him to stay busy. To keep his mind off what it worked over endlessly whenever he was alone or idle. Hell, he'd owe Justin a hell of a lot more than alcohol if he made the team.

Drew had wanted to be a S.E.A.L. for as long as he could remember. His father had been one, but it wasn't carrying on a family tradition so much as spite for the man that drove Drew forward in pursuit of the goal. One of these days he'd show the son of a bitch that he was twice the man his father would ever be.

He'd never walk out on the mother of his children. Or marry a woman half his age. Or forget his kids even existed. And he wouldn't end up with a dishonorable discharge from the Navy, either. If Drew's entire life was defined by being what his father wasn't, then he'd be fine with that.

"Twenty-eight, twenty-nine…" Justin counted.

"I heard a rumor that command might be ordering me on R & R leave," Drew said on an exhale.

Justin didn't respond immediately. "It'll be good for you, you know," he said slowly, as if weighing each word.

"I don't want to have any extra time on my hands. Makes me crazy right now."

"So spend all day training. You're going to need it."

Drew had thought of that already. He nodded, unable to muster any words at the moment.

"Maybe you ought to get away somewhere. Take a trip down to Mexico or Hawaii. Just get the hell out of here so you're not looking at the scene every day."

He'd thought of that, too. He still had a ticket to Hawaii from a canceled vacation that he needed to use.

"Alone?" he grunted.

"Hey, man, I'd go with you if I had any leave left. What about that girl you were dating? Tanya? Tawny?"

"We weren't a couple, and it ain't happening."

"You stopped seeing her?"

"Ages ago. No chemistry."

Justin watched him for a while, counting. Then he said, "I guess everyone's being given R & R, right?"

"So rumor goes."

"You ever notice how Lieutenant Commander Thomas looks at you?"

"No."

"Like she wants to have you for dinner. Maybe you ought to take *her* on vacation."

"She's my freaking boss, asshole."

Justin shrugged. "So what? What happens on R & R is your own business. And no one's gonna blame you for dealing with your grief however you need to."

"Don't be such a prick."

"All right, all right. Sorry. I just think there's something intriguing about that woman."

"I've never noticed."

"Fair enough. But I tell ya, man, if she ever looked at me the way she looks at you, I'd be all over her. Screw rank."

Drew tuned out Justin's comment. Between training and the shooting, seducing his boss was the last thing on his mind right now—or at any other time, for that matter. Besides, regardless of what Justin said, Lieutenant Commander Thomas had never treated him as anything other than a subordinate under her command. She was career Navy and he'd lay odds she wasn't even capable of action outside the code of conduct.

He grimaced as his abs and lats began to burn.

"Hey, you know," Justin said, "I've got a diver buddy who runs a school in Honolulu. I could hook you up with him for a little extreme training if you head out that way."

"Not a bad idea." Drew blinked at the sweat dripping into his eyes, then closed them as he pushed onward.

If the rumor mill was correct and mandatory R & R was forced on his ass, he'd go to Hawaii. It sounded like as good a place to recuperate as he could think of. And the extra dive training along with a ramped-up workout regime might be enough to distract him.

Hell, he might even be exhausted enough to sleep at night.

DREW SAT AT THE BAR next to Justin and did his best not to notice the people crowding the place. He didn't want to talk, didn't want to smile, didn't want to do anything but down a few triple shots of Jameson and get lost in the whiskey's sweet, warm haze. Going out for drinks had been Justin's idea, and it had sounded like a good one to Drew when the alternative was being totally alone.

He was exhausted from his workout. On top of that he hadn't slept for more than an hour last night. Not exactly prime socializing condition, but he couldn't imagine going home alone right now. He didn't want to be in an empty house with nothing but his tortured thoughts to entertain him.

He'd come to think of his constant state of agitation as an adrenaline hangover. Same way he'd felt two years ago during the war in Iraq.

Same as it never was.

Justin caught the bartender's eye and they both placed their orders, then they sat silently, both aware of Drew's morose mood. Drew pretended to be interested in the game on the flat-screen TV across the room. But he saw little more than color and motion. Nothing else registered. He wasn't numb inside. More like numb on the outside while internally, he felt a raging torrent threatening to escape.

He'd seen a friend die in action, but that was war. That was different. He hadn't ever gone into the office in peaceful, easygoing, no-worries San Diego expecting to see his coworkers mowed down by gunfire.

Damn. That train of thought went nowhere good. To distract himself he scanned the room. His gaze landed on a familiar figure near the door.

Justin spotted her only a moment after Drew. He nudged him with his elbow. "Hey, if it isn't the very woman we were talking about before."

Drew ignored him. But he couldn't ignore Justin's earlier comment about how Kylie watched him and how Justin would jump her given the chance. Without even intending to, Drew wondered how good in bed she'd be. Would she issues orders directing his performance? Or would she drop the whole officer demeanor and let loose?

On that tempting thought he took a good look at her out of uniform. Her strawberry-blond hair glinted in the light from the jukebox next to her, and her pale skin and green eyes seemed illuminated. Drew had never really thought of her as attractive, though she clearly was. It wouldn't be a hardship getting busy with her.

What was he doing? He muttered a curse. She was still his boss and no less inaccessible than she'd been this afternoon. Damn Justin for even putting this stupid idea in his head.

He glanced her way one last time.

How *had* she been looking at him?

"She wants you, man. This is your chance. I'll call her over here."

"Don't bother, asshole."

She headed to the opposite side of the U-shaped bar, where no one was sitting. Kylie hung out here often enough. He'd bumped into her now and then, though she'd always been a bit cool and standoffish with him. As a commanding officer, she was good enough, but as a person, he got the impression she was a bit lacking in the heart and soul department.

Tonight she was probably hoping for the same hazy avoidance of what had happened last week as he was. And she probably wanted to find her comfort alone, just as he did. Funny how it didn't occur to either of them to hang together even though they'd been through the same ordeal.

The bartender was busy taking Kylie's drink order, but when he turned to retrieve a glass, her gaze crossed the bar and landed on Drew. He saw some emotion flicker there—fear, perhaps, or dread—then she changed her expression into something that looked more like friendliness.

Justin waved her over.

She rose from her seat and rounded the bar, then took a seat beside Drew with a sigh. "Hi, guys," she said.

"I was just telling Drew how gorgeous you look out of uniform," Justin said, his comment totally inappropriate, especially given her rank compared to theirs.

She smirked, her expression cool. She'd probably had to deal with sexual harassment in the Navy so many times that it didn't even make her blink anymore.

"Sorry I can't say the same for you," she replied.

"Ouch." He made a show of acting wounded. "I apologize, ma'am. Sometimes when I'm in the company of a truly beautiful woman, I lose all my good sense."

Okay. He was laying it on a little thick, and Drew felt an unexpected surge of jealousy. Wasn't he the one Justin thought should be flirting with Kylie?

In fact, now that she was close his thoughts circled back to her in bed. And because he was really looking, he did have to admit she was hot. Beneath her coolness, something about her gave the slightest hint that she smoldered.

He found himself suddenly wanting to find out for himself. And he wanted Justin to get the hell away from her and stop ogling her like she was a slab of beef and he was the hungry shopper.

Thankfully, after a few more minutes of Kylie shooting down his every line, Justin realized he wasn't helping matters with his flirting. He cast a meaningful glance at Drew. "If you two will excuse me," he said, picking up his drink, "I just spotted someone I need to say hello to."

And with that, he was gone.

Drew breathed a sigh of relief.

"How you doing?" he asked. Stupid. He already knew the answer was lousy, but he'd never been schooled in the art of post-mass-shooting small talk.

"I'm…alive."

"Yeah. I couldn't make myself go home to an empty house, you know?"

"I know," she said, wincing.

She waved at the confused bartender when he scanned the bar to see where she'd gone. He placed a glass of clear liquid and a lime in front of her.

"Tequila?" Drew asked.

She nodded. "Don Julio…seems appropriate for a night like this."

The one-week anniversary of the shooting.

Drew downed half his whiskey, then stared at the amber liquid as images of that day crowded his head. He wanted them all gone, so he drank the rest of the Jameson and waited for the haze to come.

The images remained.

"You did your best there, you know," he finally said, figuring she was probably at least as racked with guilt as he was. "There's nothing more you could have done."

"Yeah," she said unconvincingly. "I guess. That's what the therapist keeps telling me."

He looked over at her until she met his gaze. "I know you feel responsible because they were your people."

Her expression went from blank to crumpled with

grief, which wasn't what he'd expected. The Kylie he knew didn't show strong emotions in public. Ever.

Drew put a hand on her back as she fought to regain control, covering her face with her hands. When her hands dropped into her lap, he could see she was on the verge of bursting into tears. His gut wrenched. He supposed even ice queens had to grieve, but he should not have felt so stricken by her emotion. After all, he was grieving, too.

"I can't get any of it out of my head. If I let myself think about it, I see the scene unfold over and over again. Only in slow motion, which makes me think of all the things I could have done. It's driving me crazy."

"Same here," he said, lifting his empty glass at the bartender and nodding for another round. "Hence the whiskey."

Kylie nodded and picked up her own alcohol, swirled it around in the glass, then took one long drink that emptied it. Afterward, she exhaled and closed her eyes. An almost visible peacefulness passed over her features. Drew watched, transfixed.

Why had he never realized Kylie was a beautiful woman? He didn't usually go for girls in uniform, let alone girls in uniform as devoid of femininity as Kylie seemed. So obviously he'd never seen the standard issues.

And yet, looking at her now, he could see something he'd missed. For one thing, she looked vulnerable. Not the invincible admiral-to-be that she behaved like at work, but a real, flesh-and-blood woman. And when her face showed emotion, she seemed pretty in a way he couldn't have guessed. Beautiful like storm clouds, like angry surf.

It didn't hurt that she wasn't in uniform right now. She was wearing a black tank top that hugged her slender curves and a pair of jeans that he couldn't help noticing did the same when he let his gaze drop below her face.

Whoa. Did he just check out his boss? This was Lieutenant Commander Thomas he was having less-than-pure thoughts about, not any old girl in a bar. It was one thing to speculate about her as he had when she showed up at the bar. It was something else entirely to sit beside her and imagine how she'd look after he peeled off that top and got his hands on what was actually an impressive rack now that it wasn't covered by a sexless uniform. He'd bet she had a tight bod—

Damn it. He was doing it again. Entertaining inappropriate thoughts about her. He reminded himself that she assessed his work performance and if he screwed up by offending her, she could deep-six his career in zero seconds flat. But even that sobering thought didn't completely stop the sexual journey his mind was on. Man, what was with him tonight? Must be the grief. Or pain avoidance. Or Justin's innuendo. Or maybe the Jameson was turning him into a mental perv.

"What?" she asked.

He realized he was staring dumbly at his boss like a love-struck schoolboy. Great.

"Oh, nothing. I just—" *What? Was thinking how damn hot you are when you're not being an uptight commander?* "I was just wondering if you knew whether we were getting a forced R & R."

"Officially, no. But it wouldn't surprise me. Kind of like the counseling, R & R seems to be the commanders' way of dealing with us." She paused, as if contemplating the situation. "You know, it's the last thing I want right now—to have a bunch of time on my hands to think about things."

"My thoughts exactly."

"So if the orders come down, what are you going to do?"

"I'll probably head to Hawaii. Throw myself into training for the S.E.A.L. test."

"Sounds like the perfect distraction." She caught the bartender's eye and motioned for another drink.

Drew made a mental note to watch out for her and make sure she got a cab home. Someone with her slender build surely couldn't handle too many shots of tequila before things would start to get messy.

"What about you?" he asked. "Any idea what you'd do with the time off?"

"Go crazy."

"You might want to make a more specific plan than that."

Before he could pursue the subject further, Justin rejoined them.

"Hey, something's come up—" he nodded toward a cute brunette hovering near the door "—so I'm outta here. You coming with?"

"Nah. I'm good here." Drew wasn't ready to leave Kylie. Someone had to make sure no one took advantage of her, right?

"All right, then. Lieutenant Commander, a pleasure to see you. Next time I'll keep my senses and show you a much better time than this guy." Kylie rolled her eyes at his boast. "I'll catch up with you at the next workout session," he said to Drew with a slap on the back. Justin walked away, pausing to give Drew a thumb's-up behind Kylie's back. Drew ignored him.

An awkward silence descended.

He marveled at how odd it felt to be sitting here with Lieutenant Commander Thomas, of all people. She'd never talked to him much at work, except to give orders or instructions, and she was always noticeably cold and distant. Now, though, she seemed like a normal woman.

And what had changed? The shooting, of course. If he had to guess, he'd say she'd been humbled by it. The day of the shooting was the first time he'd ever seen her shaken. And that had been the first time he'd realized she was more than just a pencil-pushing officer. In her refusal to escape while she had the chance and her determination to face Caldwell, she'd demonstrated a selfless desire to protect her subordinates. She'd revealed herself to be a true leader who cared about her people and would lay down her life to keep them from harm. It had been a glimpse behind the ladder-climbing officer who played everything by the book and kept everyone at arm's length.

"Why are you looking at me like that?" she said.

He'd had enough to drink that he didn't consider telling anything but the truth. "I was just thinking how brave you were last week, and how if I had to have a leader to go to war with, I'd choose you."

She stared at him for a long time. "Thank you," she

finally said. "I'm not sure I deserve kudos for bravery, but I appreciate you saying it. Really you were the one who saved us from getting shot. I haven't shared how grateful I am for that, but I really do want to say it. Thank you for saving my life."

Drew shook his head. "I didn't do enough. I failed the people who died that day."

Kylie sighed. "That's exactly how I feel. I can think of dozens of actions I should have taken. But your actions were heroic. You have to believe that."

Drew stared at his glass, unwilling to accept her words but not wanting to seem ungracious by arguing any further.

When she placed a hand on his arm, his entire body went on red alert and all his dirty thoughts about her crowded his brain. He'd never have expected her touch to affect him that way.

"Hey," she said, her tone noticeably lighter now. "Will you help me pick some songs from the jukebox? If I have to hear 'Love Shack' one more time, I'm going to start a bar fight."

Drew couldn't help but smile. "Sure, why not."

She stood and he watched her begin walking toward the jukebox. He caught sight of exactly how well her jeans fit her, hugging her ass and accentuating her narrow waist in a way that should have been criminal. An image of the two of them together, their naked limbs tangled together, formed. Kylie's long wavy hair—now freed from the stiff bun she wore at work to cascade down her back—splayed across the pillow. Her delicious ass was cupped in his hands and he buried himself deep inside her.

He fought to banish the lustful image, but it seemed burned on his mind's screen. His boss wasn't just pretty, she was downright smoking hot. So hot, in fact, that if she propositioned him right here, right now, he'd have her bent over the bar before she finished the sentence. Forget the Navy. Forget his career. Burying himself in Kylie seemed worth the cost.

The intensity of his attraction to her blew him away. He knew himself well enough to know that a reaction this strong had something to it. This wasn't grief or Justin's innuendo or the Jameson. Sure, those things might have opened his eyes to the possibility, but his desire was real.

The only question was, what would he do about it?

3

SOMEWHERE BETWEEN her third and fourth shots of Don Julio, Kylie's worries slipped away. She also conveniently forgot why she'd ever been so resistant to indulging her attraction to Drew.

After her fifth shot, she leaned over to kiss him on the cheek, a gesture she'd thought of as comforting, a way to emphasize their newfound camaraderie and perhaps bring him out of his funk. But he turned his head at the last second, and her kiss landed on his lips.

This was a turn of events, so to speak, that she had not anticipated. Things got really interesting when, instead of reacting with shock and pulling away, he kissed her back.

Really kissed her back.

And that was the beginning of the end of their propriety. They both seemed intent on the same goal. There wasn't any question of what was going to happen, on either of their parts.

"Want to catch a cab?" he said when they finally broke apart. It seemed a foregone conclusion they would spend a night in each other's arms.

Ten minutes later, they were all over each other in the back of a taxi. Drew's hands were between her legs, under her shirt, inside her pants…everywhere she wanted them to be. Still she could think of nothing but how badly she wanted more. She'd been dreaming about getting busy with Drew for the past year and it had been twice that long since she'd been with a man. A pure, intense need for sex was driving her. That and the delicious things Drew's mouth was doing.

Somewhere in the back of her mind, the leader in her was making excuses for her potentially career-ending behavior. This was a typical reaction to tragedy. The desire to be a part of life and the living was a healthy way to cope with death, and what better way to feel a part of life than to have sex with someone?

The rest of Kylie wasn't arguing.

She was only vaguely aware of the presence of the cabdriver. So what if he was getting off on watching them make out? She was too caught up in the feel of Drew's body against hers to care about anything else now.

The cab stopped at what she could only assume was Drew's house, and he paid the driver, and then they were alone on a cool, dark lawn, illuminated only by the faint glow of a porch light. Kylie wasn't sure who first fell down on the grass, but once they were both rolling around, kissing, struggling to remove clothing, gasping for breath in their urgency to continue what they'd started, it really didn't matter.

Her head was spinning in a mildly pleasant way that made her feel as though she were in a movie again, the camera circling and circling the frenzy of their activity. Everything was in soft focus for her, except for the intense need that propelled her.

She was naked now, her back against the damp grass, her clothes scattered nearby. She was pretty sure she'd never been naked in public before. Not like this anyway. In the back of her mind, the ever-so-proper Naval officer filed a complaint against this lewd and inappropriate behavior. Thanks to the tequila flowing in her veins, Kylie was able to ignore that uptight prude and concentrate on riding this pleasure trip as far as it would take her.

Drew—bless him for being prepared—had produced a condom and was sliding it onto himself.

And wow, he was naked, too. Gloriously so—his body a wonderland of sculpted muscle and smooth flesh she couldn't stop her hands from exploring.

Then he was on top of her. Then he was inside her. Yes, that was it—inside her, exactly where she needed him to be. She spread her legs and moaned softly into his ear as he stretched her from within, reaching places that had gone sadly neglected for far too long, awakening nerve endings that cried out for stimulation.

She almost came at the sheer relief of being filled up by a man again. There was nothing, absolutely nothing, like the sensation of cradling a man's—this man's—hips within her own.

And then he was moving inside her, his hot, hard body pressed against her, her legs wrapped around his waist as she took him in.

Her head was still spinning, even more pleasantly now.

Time folded in on itself, and she was aware only of the tangle of their limbs, the frantic movements of their lovemaking, the hot dampness of Drew's mouth against hers. Then his mouth caressed her neck, then on to her aching, neglected breasts…and lower still. He withdrew his cock, but before she could protest, his lips nibbled across her belly, down her thigh, and there, *yes*… She gasped as he moved between her legs and began coaxing her toward climax with his tongue.

It didn't take much. She'd already been humming with pent-up desire, and what seemed like only a few strokes of his clever tongue sent her over the edge, crying out at the intensity of her orgasm.

Her inner muscles were still quaking when he covered her with his body again and penetrated her, pumping hard as he brought himself to climax. In a matter of seconds he was there, and the intensity of it gave her a second orgasm on the heels of her first.

She was spiraling upward, breathless, crying out, her body a quivering mass of raw sensation as Drew moaned against her cheek and filled her with a few final, spent thrusts.

She'd never come twice in a row before. This roll on the grass had ranked in her personal top five and all it had taken was a bit of exhibitionism, a man she'd fantasized about endlessly and a few shots of tequila to drop her inhibitions. Even as drunk as she was, she couldn't help but marvel at becoming a multiple-O girl.

Why was she surprised? If any man had the talent to make her come more than twice, it would be Drew. He was everything she'd imagined in her fantasies, and then some. For such a young guy, he was a skilled lover…or at least it seemed so after five shots of tequila.

As much as she wanted to wallow in those two

orgasms, reality started to intrude. The damp grass was cold and itchy. And Drew was heavy. And parts of him dug into her in ways she shifted to avoid.

They roused themselves and made their way out of his front yard and into his house. And once inside, round two proved that the multiple-O version of Kylie was not a one-hit wonder.

KYLIE LAY AWAKE in the dark, her gaze fixed on the ceiling. They had been asleep for a few hours, maybe more—she couldn't be sure how much time had passed since she didn't see a clock from her vantage point and didn't feel quite well enough to sit up and look for one.

She was drunk enough to know she shouldn't attempt to drive home, but sober enough to realize she'd just made a huge, potentially career-ending mistake.

She'd just slept with her subordinate. What the hell had she been thinking? Did all of her effort, all of her sweat and grim determination to climb the ranks mean so little to her that a bit—okay, maybe more than a bit—of alcohol demoed her control and made her so reckless?

Dear God, she'd really done it. She'd acted out the fantasies that had plagued her ever since she'd first laid eyes on Ensign MacLeod. And, yes, rolling around on his lawn—lord, please let the neighbors have been in bed—then tangling in his sheets, was every bit as good as she'd imagined it would be. It was so good that she found herself wanting to linger in the hope that they'd have a repeat performance before daylight came and exposed her indiscretions.

For the first time she could remember in her career, she was seeing a glimpse of the shameful woman she might have become. The one who couldn't control her impulses, the one whose passions outran her discipline, the one who took what she wanted without considering the consequences. That's the kind of girl she'd been. But thanks to some crappy circumstances, at the age of seventeen she'd made the conscious decision to lay that impulsive girl to rest and never let her live again.

She squeezed her eyes shut at the thought, fighting back tears.

She'd become, instead, the woman her strict, God-fearing Iowa farming parents had wanted her to be. Their voices lurked in the back of her head, chiding her whenever she felt the urge to stray from their narrow idea of right and wrong, reminding her of how much she'd almost screwed up her life by following her passions. And for a long time, she'd thought she'd made the right choice in following their rules, and then the Navy's. She'd become the woman everyone else seemed to want her to be, a woman they could be proud of.

But for the past week, her whole life seemed to be in question. She'd begun to suspect it was a total sham. That following everyone else's codes and standards wasn't the secret of her success, but rather the prison that prevented her from following her dreams.

It was strange how the shooting had forced her to confront her own mortality in a way that combat never had. Maybe because it was her job to risk her life fighting for freedom and her country. Maybe because she believed any danger she faced was worth supporting the greater good. The shooting, by comparison, was senseless, serving only to assuage one man's ego and thirst for vengeance.

If life could disappear in the blink of an eye, if any moment could truly be her last, then why was she living the way she was? Why was her career the only thing she had to show for her life? Why was she still, as a woman well into her thirties, looking for the approval of her parents and her superiors at work? Why was she so carefully walking her straight-and-narrow path, not daring to give in to any temptation?

She looked over at Drew sleeping. Somehow he had come to represent everything she'd denied herself. Passion, love, joy…

Why was she living for things that didn't really matter if she died tomorrow?

She couldn't produce any answers to her questions, but she knew she didn't want to live that way anymore.

And yet, reality was creeping in as the sky outside began turning from black to gray. Soon it would be morning. Soon she'd have to face the fact that she'd just slept with her subordinate and she wouldn't be able to wrap up the fallout in I-want-to-be-me rhetoric. She would have to face him every day in the office. She'd have to issue his orders, evaluate his performance and administer any discipline while pretending that she didn't know how good he looked naked and how delicious he tasted. She was pretty sure he could keep things discreet, that he would have just as much incentive as she to act as though nothing had happened between them.

The problem was, she didn't want to act as though

nothing had happened. She wanted to yell from the
rooftop that she'd finally done what she'd been longing to do, that she loved Drew MacLeod, and she
wasn't going to deny it anymore.

Loved?

That was a strong word. But perhaps not a totally
inaccurate one. Maybe what she was feeling was
lust or infatuation. Whatever label she put on her
emotion, it hadn't lessened after having her way with
Drew. If anything, it was more intense and looking
a lot more like love.

Okay, no. She was really, really drunk. These crazy
thoughts were just the tequila combined with a big dose
of grief talking. She needed to get a grip and figure out
how she was going to handle this disaster she'd created.

She needed to think…think…think…

But damn it, her head was starting to pound. She
closed her eyes and willed the sensation to disappear.
A little pain reliever was called for. Except, before
she could even think where Drew might keep the
aspirin, a wave of nausea hit her. It went quickly
from being a mere wave to being the certainty that
she was going to throw up.

She shot up from the bed and ran to the nearest door
praying it hid the bathroom. Luckily it did, because
the motion of jumping up and running across the room
had done her in. The moment she knelt beside the
toilet, she lost her dinner from the night before, along
with everything she'd eaten for the past month. Or so
it seemed to her aching body.

Afterward, she could only sag in relief. She wiped
tears from her eyes that had come with the onslaught.

Drew must have heard her miserable retching. "Are you okay?" he asked from the doorway.

"No," she muttered, her forehead resting on her arms against the toilet seat. "I'm dying."

"I'll get you some water and aspirin."

She could hear him moving around in the small bathroom, but misery mixed with humiliation kept her from raising her head. This was so not a cool way to end a night of amazing sex. The last thing she wanted was for Drew to see her at her absolute worst.

After a few moments, she felt his hand on the back of her head, rubbing gently.

"You drank a lot."

"No kidding."

"It might help to eat something."

Kylie moaned, the thought of food none too pleasing right now.

"I know it doesn't sound good, but I'll make you a little breakfast."

"No, please…" she said, but he was gone.

She listened as his footsteps got farther and farther away. Then she could hear him banging around in the kitchen.

Slowly, the remnants of her nausea disappeared, and she was left with only her pounding head. She couldn't keep sitting here naked on the bathroom floor, so she cautiously stood, rinsed her mouth out, then downed the aspirin and water he'd left for her.

In the bedroom again, she wondered if she was up to getting dressed and leaving. But no, they needed to talk, and it would be cowardly to rush out of there, given the magnitude of what they'd done. Besides, she wasn't sure if her clothes were inside or still scattered about his lawn.

Oh, dear god, his *lawn*. Had they really done that? Had they even waited until the cabbie had driven away to start stripping each other down and getting it on? Thankfully she couldn't remember. That particular time, when the alcohol must have been hitting her hardest, was all a pleasant, hazy blur.

She spotted a robe hanging from a closet door and put it on before lying down on the bed again to wait out her headache.

Whatever else happened, she mused, at least she knew now that if she died tomorrow, she had acted out her greatest fantasy.

That was a comforting thought…sort of.

4

DREW SAT on the edge of the bed next to Kylie, who was dozing quietly. Even hungover, she looked beautiful in the pale morning light. He reached out to brush a strand of honey-colored hair off her cheek, then thought better of it for fear of waking her.

The effects of the whiskey had worn off for him, and he had avoided feeling as awful as Kylie had. The warm buzz of the alcohol had been replaced by a different kind of warm buzz—an unexpected affection for this woman he'd never given a second glance.

This was a different woman than the one he knew as his commander. This Kylie was vulnerable and passionate and real. She was the woman he'd just had the best sex of his life with. She captivated him, intrigued him, made him want more.

Something momentous had happened between them. Okay, maybe it had been fueled by booze. But in his experience, alcohol only lubricated the way for things people really wanted to do. It didn't make anyone do anything they were totally opposed to. And clearly he wasn't opposed to doing Kylie…again and again.

Twenty-four hours ago, if anyone had suggested to him he'd be having a night of crazy monkey sex with his lieutenant commander, he'd have sworn they were nuts. And if they suggested he'd be considering a future with her the next morning, he might have run for the hills. He recalled his conversation with Justin the day before and shook his head. Sometimes friends really did know better than anyone what was best for a person.

Drew and Kylie would have to keep their relationship under wraps for a while since she was his C.O. So they'd have to play it cool in public and sneak around—which could be hot. Once he passed the S.E.A.L. test and moved out from under her command, however, they were good to go. It was a sudden shift for him to go from not noticing her to figuring out how to fit her in his life. But he'd learned to run with his instincts, and they were telling him what he shared with Kylie was real.

She shifted in her sleep, and the blanket slid off her shoulder, revealing her beautiful round breasts in the open neck of his robe. Drew had never noticed that she even had much of a chest, she did such a good job of hiding it under her uniform. Damn, did she ever have one of the nicest sets of tits he'd ever laid eyes on. It took all his willpower not to reach out and caress them right then.

Instead he pulled the blanket back up to cover her. The disturbance woke her and she looked at him through half-closed eyes, a frown on her face.

"How long have I been sleeping?"

"Fifteen or twenty minutes. Feel any better?"

"Yeah, my head's not pounding as much—I guess the aspirin kicked in."

"How about some breakfast in bed?"

"No, I can get up." She started to rise, but he placed a hand on her lap to stop her.

"Stay," he said in a tone that ended the argument. "You shouldn't be exerting yourself right now."

She sank into her pillow and shrugged, a slight smile playing on her lips.

Drew went to the kitchen, grabbed the tray of toast, scrambled eggs, melon, juice and coffee he'd already prepared, and returned with it. Nothing fancy, but it was good, simple hangover fare meant to soothe the stomach more than dazzle the taste buds.

Kylie regarded him with something like awe when he placed the tray on her lap. "Thank you so much," she said. "I'm not sure how much I can eat, but this is… heavenly. I've never been served breakfast in bed before."

"No? How could that be?"

"Well, unless I count eating a bowl of cereal alone in my own bed."

"That just sounds sad. Breakfast in bed, by definition, has to be served to you by someone else."

She adjusted herself against the headboard and sighed. "Thank you. This is really wonderful."

"I'll be right back."

Drew returned with his own cup of coffee and toast and slid into bed beside her.

"This is a lot of food. Want to share?"

"Sure, I'll eat a little," he said, swiping a piece of melon.

She ate silently for a few minutes, taking little bites as if she were testing her body's ability to ingest anything.

She put down her fork and regarded him solemnly. "Listen," she said, "I'm really sorry about what happened last night. Clearly things got out of control, and—"

"Please stop. You don't need to apologize for anything. We were both consenting adults." He wasn't sure he wanted to hear her apologize as if she regretted what had been a life-altering experience for him. He still needed a little time to process what had happened before he dove into talking about his feelings and their future. It all needed to be clearer in his head before they could talk about where they'd go from here.

And, yeah, since the night had been fueled by alcohol, he wanted to give her some time to recover from her hangover.

"True, but we're consenting adults who are a part of the same unit, and we have to consider..." She paused.

"We have to consider what?" he asked, his instincts sensing he was about to hear something he wouldn't like.

She took a deep breath and continued. "Obviously we have to consider how our careers could be impacted by our behavior. I want to make it clear that this won't affect any of our interactions at work."

"Of course it will," he blurted. "I mean, how could it not?"

She blinked, and he could see her cheeks turn red. When she spoke again, it was with much deliberation.

"I'm very aware that I'm your superior. I am in a precarious position because I can't allow sleeping with you to affect how I evaluate your work performance. More than that, if anyone found out about this, about us, I could lose my career."

Drew's stomach turned at her words. He'd been thinking about what a momentous event this had been in his life, and all she could worry about was how it might affect her goddamn career?

"I don't know what to say. If you're worried about me telling people, don't. I won't say a word."

"Thank you," she said, visibly relieved, and he felt then as if she'd kicked him in the gut.

"Sure, don't mention it," he said a bit too churlishly, and she looked at him curiously.

"Are you bothered by what I said?"

"How could I not be? I don't like being considered your drunken mistake or a potential threat to your career."

She blushed a deeper red. "I'm sorry. I mean, I thought you'd understand that obviously, we can't let this go any further than last night."

"I get it," he said.

"No matter how great it was," she added, as if that might smooth things over.

"Yeah, right."

She looked at her food like she couldn't swallow another bite. Drew didn't have much of an appetite now himself. He dropped the toast on his nightstand beside his neglected cup of coffee and lay down, his head spinning now.

Had he fabricated the woman from last night? No, he hadn't. But why had he dared to think the hard-ass Lieutenant Commander Thomas was a different woman from the Kylie who sat with him at the bar?

He was naive, that's why. She had nearly a decade on him when it came to putting her career above all else. Which explained why she was always alone, had never had a boyfriend for as long as he'd known her, as far as he could tell. Then again, maybe her M.O. was getting loaded, picking up guys, then giving them the brush-off after she'd screwed their brains out.

She set aside her tray and rolled onto her side, placing a hand on his shoulder. "I've upset you," she said, stating the obvious.

Great. He was clearly acting like a pouting child, drawing attention to the age difference between them—which, until this moment, hadn't been a big deal to him. Well, he didn't give a damn, because he wasn't about to separate his heart from how he lived his life. If there was anything he'd learned from the past few years, it was that life was fleeting. You had to appreciate the things that mattered and chase after the things you wanted while you had the chance.

"I thought I felt a real connection between us."

She bit her lip, regarding him with a mixture of embarrassment and earnestness. "You did. I mean, of course you did. But I think that's partly because we endured a major life trauma together. Like the shrink says, it makes sense that we'd seize upon something good and life-affirming in the face of tragedy."

"If it's so good and life-affirming, then why do we have to pretend it didn't happen?"

"You know why. The Navy expects us to put what's good for our country ahead of what might be good for us personally. We accepted that when we became officers. And nothing good can come of a commander sleeping with her subordinate, as far as the Navy is concerned."

Drew said nothing, his pride still wounded.

He didn't want her writing off what had happened between them as purely the result of their having endured a tragedy together. It hadn't been that way for him and he didn't want it to have been that way for her. When he'd gotten over the tightness in his throat, he spoke without considering his words. "Last week wasn't the first time I've been through grim circumstances. I've been to war, and two years ago, I lost my sister—my best friend—to cancer."

"I'm sorry," she whispered.

"My point is, I can tell the difference between an emotional response to tragedy, and a real genuine connection with another person."

"We don't get to pursue every emotional connection we feel with another person."

"Neither of us is married, or involved with anyone else, right?"

"Right, but—"

"I don't believe in putting my career above all else. I just can't live my life that way."

It was her turn to be silent. She looked away from him toward the window where the orange glow of sunrise was showing.

Drew wondered how true his words really were. He'd sacrificed a lot for his career so far. And if he made the S.E.A.L. team as he hoped, he'd be sacrificing a lot more. Was he really so different from Kylie?

"Tell me about your sister," she finally said. "I mean, if you don't mind. I'd like to know what she was like."

He'd learned everything he needed to know about life from watching the most important person in his life die: love fiercely, take nothing for granted and never for a second make the mistake of thinking life is fair.

Enough time had passed. He'd finally gotten to a point where thinking about Abby didn't make him unbearably sad. He could remember all that was good about her now, and he held on to those memories for dear life.

"Her name was Abby. We were close growing up because our mother was a wreck, and we didn't have much choice but to take care of each other."

"Was your dad around?"

"Not for long. He bailed when I was six, and my mom never recovered. She went looking for the answer to her troubles at the bottom of a wine bottle, and things kept falling further and further apart."

She listened, not offering any unnecessary condolences.

"Abby was a serious person, but she had a silly side that I brought out of her. She was four years older than me, and she is probably the main reason I've made anything of my life. She looked out for me when no one else did, and she made sure I did well in school, got into college and stayed on track."

"And she died just two years ago?"

Drew nodded. "Exactly a year after she found out she had breast cancer. It seemed like the most unfair thing in the world that could ever happen. It still does."

"It must have been hell to watch her go through that."

"The worst part was, I'd finished college, gotten my commission and went straight to Iraq. I couldn't even be with her most of that final year."

"Oh God, I'm sorry."

"She sent me Web cam photos of herself wasting away. She had a sick sense of humor sometimes, and she was always making jokes about her hair falling out and stuff."

"You must still feel the loss," Kylie said, looking at him earnestly. It touched him that she really seemed to empathize.

He said nothing, but instead cast his gaze toward the window and the sunrise.

He'd never cried on anyone's shoulder, and he really had mourned the loss of his sister past the point of her memory still being painful. But right now he could have curled up beside Kylie and cried himself a pool of tears on the pillow.

Part of him loved that Kylie managed to bring out such strong feelings in him, even while part of him braced for the return of Lieutenant Commander Thomas.

He wasn't sure if he'd been fooling himself about the woman he thought he'd glimpsed in her last night—or if the alcohol had colored his view—but the woman watching him now with so much soulfulness in her eyes was definitely the Kylie he wanted to know better.

5

KYLIE COULD NOT have been a bigger jerk. She had let the misery of her hangover and her fear of the consequences get in the way of any sensitivity with which she might have handled the situation, and in her callousness she'd likely done irreparable damage. She knew exactly what Drew felt last night, because she felt it, too. There'd been something incredibly intense about their coming together, something that, in another time and place, might have promised so much more.

She looked at him stretched out next to her, wearing nothing but a pair of black boxer briefs, and she felt a rush of warmth between her legs at the sight of him. They'd had amazing sex—sex that she'd love to repeat. Not that she could imagine doing anything at the moment. Her headache might have mostly vanished, and her nausea had passed, but she still felt weak and exhausted…on top of feeling like an utter jerk for blurting out the career talk so quickly and so awkwardly.

And she'd managed to bring the mood in the room even lower by asking about his dead sister. The tone in his voice had spoken volumes about how deep his affection for Abby went. Kylie was touched by that.

Not having a sibling herself, she envied their relationship, even though he'd suffered a profound loss.

That he was mature enough to talk about it as he had also spoke volumes about his character.

"Thank you for telling me about your sister," Kylie said, rolling onto her belly and resting her chin on her hands. "I've never lost anyone like that, so I count myself lucky."

Drew said nothing, just looked thoughtful, and the silence began to weigh heavily between them, making Kylie feel like she needed to fill the space with words.

But what?

She sensed that he didn't want to share any more personal stuff right now, and she didn't see the point of getting more intimate. That direction led to a relationship and the only relationship in their future was a professional one. If she brought up the career impact issue again, she'd only insult him further. If she tried to reassure him she did indeed feel the spark between them, she'd sound as fake as she had earlier.

"I wish the circumstances between us were different," she finally said, bracing herself for the fallout.

He simply looked over at her and sighed. "Me, too," he said without any anger or resentment.

Good. Maybe he had come to terms with reality and wasn't going to make any further noise about pursuing a connection. Maybe they could navigate this situation smoothly, and no one's career would have to suffer.

Kylie, for the first time as an officer, found herself feeling the unpleasant chafing of having to be the responsible, upright one when she would have preferred to flout the rules. She'd gone along with the Navy's idea of right and wrong for so long—since the age of eighteen when she entered the Naval Academy—that she'd ceased to question it. But now…

Now she was thinking and acting like a fool, and she needed to get out of this much younger subordinate's bed before she did anything else profoundly stupid for the sake of a little sex. Albeit fabulous sex.

"Are you finished with this?" Drew said, nodding at the tray of food she'd set aside.

"Yes. Thanks for that. It was good even if I didn't do it justice."

"Don't mention it." He rose, and Kylie watched as he took the food and drinks back to the kitchen.

She needed to get out of here. ASAP.

Tentatively she rolled over and sat up, doing her best not to upset her equilibrium. So far, so good. She went to the bathroom to clean up. When she finished and came back out, she found her clothes lying on the foot of Drew's bed. He was across the room getting dressed.

"I can call a cab so we can get our cars from the bar, if you're feeling up to it."

"Good idea," Kylie said. "I should be getting home. I have to go into the office. With everything that's been going on and the counseling and stuff, I've got tons to catch up on."

"Yeah, me, too, boss." Drew zipped up his pants and sat on the edge of the bed to put on his shoes.

Kylie bit her lip to keep from reacting to the *boss* comment, which was not only inappropriate, but also technically disrespectful, since if he was going to refer to her in a work context, he was supposed to call her

ma'am. Of course, they'd already piled inappropriateness on top of inappropriateness, so now was no time
to be a stickler for the rules. She forced herself not to
watch him, either, as tempting as the sight of him
without a shirt on was.

Instead she found her own shoes that Drew had
placed on the floor near the bed and started to put them
on, then thought better of it when she felt herself
growing queasy again.

"I think I need to lie down for a bit," she mumbled
as Drew picked up the telephone.

"Are you sure you're up for a cab ride right now?"
he asked as he waited on the phone.

"I'll be fine."

He put in the request, then hung up and sat on the
opposite side of the bed. "They'll be here in about
fifteen minutes. Why don't you rest? I'll let you know
when it's time to go."

Kylie was too weak and tired to do anything but go
along with that plan. "Thanks," she said, wishing that
she'd had the good sense not to drink so much.

What on earth had she been thinking?

Oh, right. She'd been trying not to think. That was
the problem.

And then she remembered what she'd been trying not
to think about. At least she'd accomplished that goal.

Her gut wrenched as her mind skirted thoughts of
the shooting. She closed her eyes and forced her mind
in a different direction. As usual visions of Drew filled
her head, only this time reality mixed with fantasy in
a steamy combination. Images of her limbs wrapped
around his, of him over her, under her, pressing his

cock deep inside her, of sheets tangling around them, locking them together, collided in the brain. Hotter than her hottest fantasy, she couldn't resist letting herself taste him again.

Then Drew's voice interrupted her private film clips with news of the cab's arrival. Kylie opened her eyes, realized she'd dozed off and sat up. She wasn't sure how much time had passed, but thank God, the cab was here. She could get as far away from Drew as possible.

They rode in stiff silence to the bar, and once there, Kylie was relieved when Drew didn't make a big deal of saying goodbye. They'd see each other in a few hours at the office anyway.

But as she was driving home, Kylie realized she did not want to return to an empty condo. The closer to her street she got, the stronger her stomach rebelled. She didn't want to hear the echo of her own footsteps on the hardwood floor, or see the dishes from yesterday's breakfast still in the sink waiting for her.

She'd relished living alone ever since she'd escaped the roommate deal first through dorm life at the Naval Academy, then during her years as an ensign, when shared accommodations were practically a necessity on that pay scale. She'd grown to hate navigating the minefields of household chores, bathroom time and overnight guests. Having her own space had been pure decadence after those experiences and she'd basked in having to answer to no one except herself. At the moment, however, answering to herself—not to mention facing herself in the mirror—was the problem. And it wasn't something she could avoid through the distraction of a roommate.

Nope. Her wild indiscretion and her worries over how it would all play out at work loomed. And tag teaming thoughts of work was the echo of gunfire in her head, the screams of her coworkers. A punishing soundtrack for the horrific images of those who'd been shot on the floor of her office. It was unbearable.

She pulled into her assigned parking spot under the carport at her condo. She couldn't go inside. No matter how loud she turned on the stereo or TV, she wouldn't be able to drown out the noise and the pictures in her head. There was no getting away from herself in a place filled with her. She couldn't be home alone right now. But she had nowhere else to go on a Tuesday morning with her hair still disheveled from sleep and wearing last night's clothes. She had to get cleaned up, put on her uniform and pretend everything was okay for another day.

Even if she made it through today, she still had to figure out how to make it through tomorrow, and the day after that, and the day after that, and…

Coping should have gotten easier in the time since the shooting. Instead everything was feeling more and more out of control, as if she couldn't handle one more thing. Hence, her indiscretion.

Maybe having companionship last night had only highlighted for her in big, bold letters how much she didn't want to be alone.

Maybe she should use some of her accrued vacation time to go back to Iowa to visit her parents. Or go up to Washington to visit friends. Or take a friend on a trip somewhere warm and tropical where she could simply lie on the beach for a few weeks and get lost in a paperback novel.

Kylie got out of the car, her options sounding like too much effort for too little reward in her current disconcerted, hungover state. She trudged up the sidewalk toward her door, her chest growing tighter with each step. As she reached the door, it took all her willpower not to turn around and get back in the car to drive away. She wanted to go where there would be people and noise and distraction from the turmoil inside her.

No. She couldn't be this big of a coward. She couldn't run away from herself. She couldn't flee from fear of her empty apartment, for God's sake.

She started to unlock the door, when she felt seized with panic. Her hand shook, and she couldn't turn the key.

She closed her eyes, took a few deep breaths and held on to the door to steady herself against a sudden wave of dizziness. Again the film flashed in her mind in slow motion, each image lingering for maximum torment.

Drew pulls her into that office, telling her to crawl out the window. Caldwell bursts in, his gun aimed right at her. Ensign Brian Buckley appears, in the wrong place at the wrong time. Caldwell turns on him, firing a round. Buckley sprawls against the opposite wall of the hallway and slides to the floor, leaving a streak of blood on his way down.

More movement in the hallway.

"No!" a woman's voice cries out, and Caldwell fires again.

She catches a glimpse of light brown, wavy hair as Marianne O'Brian, Kylie's receptionist, falls.

She's frozen. Unable to act. Unable to protect a single person. When it matters most, she does nothing at all.

Drew springs into action. While Caldwell's attention is turned to the people in the hallway, Drew throws himself on the gunman, risking his life to take the man down. They grapple for control. Drew gets his hands on the gun and jabs Caldwell in the head with the end of it.

Drew is on his feet, gun aimed at Caldwell as sirens outside announce the arrival of the military police.

And still, Kylie does nothing.

Later, an MP pries her hand off the edge of the windowsill and leads her out of the office. To exit the building she must walk past the bodies of the victims. She sees their dying and lifeless faces. She begins to make a low, keening sound that eventually causes the paramedics to wrap her up in a blanket and treat her for shock. Trial by carnage and she fails.

Kylie opened her eyes. She wasn't at the scene of the shooting. She was at her own front door, forehead pressed against the wood, unable to go inside.

Her face was wet...she'd been crying. Her heart still pounded, and her breath was ragged.

She tried to collect her thoughts, figure out what to do next, and her hand went instinctively for her cell phone in her purse. But who could she call, and what would she say?

Hi, I'm at my own front door and I'm afraid to open it for no apparent reason.

No, she couldn't turn this into someone else's

problem. It was her own to deal with. She had to get away. She always kept an extra uniform and an overnight pack of necessities in her trunk. She could just go to work and get herself cleaned up and dressed there. It was early, and whoever was there already wouldn't ask questions if she changed in her own office.

Her own office? Why did that place sound more comforting than her empty condo? Because there were people there.

Her mind made up, she hurried back to her car. Once inside, she realized she was going to have to calm down enough to drive safely. No easy task. Her hands were still shaking, and she was on the verge of hyperventilating. Maybe she needed to call someone after all.

No. She needed to calm down. Take some deep breaths. Exhale. Focus on the task at hand. She wasn't in any danger. She knew how to drive a car.

She could do this.

Kylie put her car in Reverse and backed out, forcing the hysteria from her mind with the mundane task of driving. She drove slowly, deliberately, around the corner, down the road, but then without thinking why, pulled over on a side street.

Now what?

Should she call Drew and tell him she was having a nervous breakdown? He, of all people, would understand. But he, of all people, was also her subordinate with whom she'd already crossed boundaries by sleeping together.

No, she had to leave him out of this. Even if everything about her life was falling apart, and she didn't know what to do next.

She gripped the steering wheel so hard her hands began to hurt. She realized what she was doing and let go. Then she was crying. Loudly. A mournful wail threatened to escape her throat. Worse, from out of nowhere, her nausea returned with a vengeance.

She had just enough time to open her car door, lean out and heave her minuscule breakfast onto the ground. When she was done, she felt some of the tension draining from her body. She fumbled around in the glove box to find a napkin, then dried her eyes and wiped her mouth.

Okay. She needed to get a grip. She leaned back in her seat, reached for the recline lever on the side of it and eased the driver's seat back a few inches. She was feeling tired now. Extremely tired.

So she would rest for a few minutes, and then she'd try again.

6

BY THE TIME Kylie made it to work, the parking lot was almost full, meaning nearly everyone else was there. So she went to the pleasantly noisy military gym a half-block away and dressed in the women's locker room. There, she didn't look out of place cleaning herself up and getting ready for work. And no one was paying close enough attention to notice that she hadn't broken a sweat from working out first.

Being surrounded by normal people going about their normal business was oddly soothing to her frazzled nerves. All that normalcy gave her hope that someday she'd rejoin that team.

When she arrived in her office five minutes late, no one took notice. That is, no one seemed to. No sooner had she settled at her desk to check her e-mail than Drew appeared in her doorway.

"Are you okay?" he said. "I was a little worried when you didn't show up earlier."

"I'm…feeling shaky, I guess."

She tried to turn her attention to her computer monitor, but it did no good. She was hyperaware of his presence now. She could torture herself with accurate images of what he looked like beneath his uniform, or better yet, memories of what he felt like pressed against her and inside her.

He stepped inside her office and closed the door, taking a liberty she was sure he wouldn't have, had they not slept together. Part of her bristled at his forwardness and lack of respect, while another part of her felt a little twinge of pleasure. Before she could stop herself, she imagined him ripping off her clothes and taking her on her own desk.

God, she needed to get a grip. She'd gone from being a woman in control of her own destiny to being one who got turned on by a guy taking charge like a brute.

She was no damsel in distress.

Or at least, she'd never seen herself as one.

Except, last week…she kind of had acted that way. And today, too, for that matter.

Her self-concept was crumbling right before her eyes.

"What can I help you with?" she asked using a no-nonsense tone to remind him—her?—who was commanding officer.

"I came by to make sure you're okay, that's all," he said, shrugging. He made no effort to leave.

She raised her eyebrows. "So now you know I am, and you can go."

"Look," he said, then stopped. And started again, "I just wanted to check in. I mean, after what happened and what we talked about. I don't want you to feel as if your reputation is at stake or anything."

Kylie's throat closed up tight. Her reputation. She never really thought about it, good or bad, especially when it came to those who reported to her. She mostly just did what was required to achieve her current goal. But Drew's words made her think of her parents. Their disapproval. Their disappointment. Her reputation was the kind of thing her father would be concerned about, would say was important.

Without thinking, she blurted, "What exactly is my reputation?"

He stared at her uncomprehendingly. "I'm sorry?"

"What do people say about me?"

"Nothing," he said too fast.

She gave him a skeptical look. "What do you think of me? As a leader?"

Why had she asked him that? It was a ridiculous question that would never get her an honest reply, anyway.

"I think you're a good leader," he said vaguely.

"Don't patronize me."

"If you're worried about last night changing how I view you at work, please don't—"

"That's not what I mean. I want to know if I'm a good officer or not, if I have weaknesses I'm not aware of, if there are things about me that make me difficult to work for."

Drew appeared to be giving the matter serious thought. Was he going to answer her honestly?

And why did she suddenly need to know so badly, anyway?

She had a feeling it was all a part of her crumbling sense of self. Some part of her was itching to smash that foundation all to bits and start over again.

"Well," he said, "if you want brutal honesty—"

"Yes, that's exactly what I want."

"I'd have to say your weakness as a leader is that you're…kind of cold. You're not really approachable when you're in uniform."

"I'm not?" she said dumbly, reeling at how honest he'd been. It was her own fault. She'd asked for it, now she had to sit here and take it. But damn, it hurt.

"It's like you separate everything that doesn't relate to the Navy and don't let it interfere with your duties. And you expect everyone else to do the same. Like you don't think anyone should have human feelings or problems that get in the way of their work."

Oh. Well. That stung.

"Don't hold back," she said sarcastically. "Go ahead with your laundry list of my faults."

He winced. "I'm sorry. Did I go too far?"

"No. I asked for it." She sighed. "But really? I'm cold and unfeeling? Difficult to approach?"

"I could be misinterpreting things," he offered, gesturing with his hands as if it wasn't such a big deal.

Yeah, too bad he hadn't misinterpreted. His words hit home because, she feared, they were spot-on accurate.

Damn it.

"The thing is," he added, "I saw a different side of you last night."

"That would be my drunken side."

"No, it wasn't just the alcohol. You're so much different when you're not the one in charge."

"What's that supposed to mean? When I'm not trying to step out of my place and wear the pants—"

"No. You're just…a hell of a lot more likable and real when you're off duty. That's all."

"Oh."

Kylie's gaze fell to her desk, and she found herself feeling truly sorry she'd initiated this discussion. She didn't need to invite a career crisis into her life at the moment. Regardless, it seemed to be coming on in and making itself at home.

"I'm sorry. I'd be happy to talk to you about it more when we're not feeling so, um, strung out or whatever."

"No, thank you. I do appreciate your honesty."

She stared at him, waiting for him to go, but he just stood there, looking as though he had something on his mind.

"Um, there's another reason I came in here," he finally said.

"Yes?"

"I was hoping you'd agree to have dinner with me. Maybe tonight or later this week. Anytime that works for you, I'll make sure I'm free."

"Oh." After the way things had ended earlier, and after his brutal honesty about how much she sucked as an officer, she definitely hadn't expected to get asked out on a date. What was he thinking? They couldn't go for dinner together. Not the two of them—commander and subordinate with one indiscretion between them already.

"I think it would do us both some good to spend time talking. You know, to someone who truly understands, I mean."

Nice try. But they both knew his invitation had

nothing to do with the shooting and everything to do with their activities on his lawn.

"No," she said. "No, I don't think that would be a good idea." Her tone implied she was done with the subject.

Drew got the message, taking a step toward the door. Then he turned back and said, "See? That's exactly what I mean. When you've got that uniform on, you act like you have no heart."

And with that, he walked out the door, leaving Kylie to mull over whether he was right, or being spiteful, or both.

KYLIE MANAGED to stumble through the next two days of work without completely losing it. But she had a feeling people around her were beginning to notice that she was officially Not Okay.

Like right now, for instance. She was supposed to be conducting the weekly staff meeting to go over the orders for everyone to take leave. Standing in front of what was left of her staff for the first time since the shooting, she was having a really hard time not bursting into tears.

"Are you okay, Lieutenant Commander?" a male voice asked, but she didn't know whose, because her vision was blurry. She sat down hard in the nearest chair.

"Would you like someone else to lead the meeting?" another voice asked.

This one she recognized as Drew's. She looked up at him. They'd barely spoken since he'd asked her out for dinner. She'd been avoiding him at every turn. Maybe...not.

Still the concern in his voice helped her regain a bit of her equilibrium. "No," she said. "I'm fine. I'll be fine."

She looked around the table, and everyone appeared uncomfortable, as if they didn't believe her. Or perhaps, they all thought their boss was a cold, icy bitch who couldn't even admit when she had real human emotions.

"This is difficult," she forced herself to say in an effort to prove she had a human side. "It's the first time we've assembled as a group here at the office since…last week. And I don't want you to feel as if we're to get back to business as usual, without my having any regard for the gravity of what we've been through.

"In fact," she went on, "I've been informed that you will be granted time for R & R, starting immediately. Those of you who have pending work issues that need to be addressed, you're to hand over any necessary files to me, and I'll delegate the work to others while you're away."

She looked around the room at the solemn faces.

Drew's expression was inscrutable, but she had a feeling he wanted to say something to her. She rushed on to fill the silence before he had a chance.

"If you have any further questions, I'll be in my office, and you may speak to me there privately. For now, you're all dismissed."

With that, she stood and left the room, her feet thankfully planting one in front of the other as they were supposed to. No sooner did she reach the safety of her own office than a male figure appeared at her door.

It was Commander Mulvany, her direct supervisor, and a man she admired for his steadfast leadership skills. He'd been a role model to her for the past few years, and it pained her to have to face him now when she was barely holding herself together.

"Lieutenant Commander, I need to speak with you in my office in five minutes," he said.

"Yes, sir," Kylie answered, her stomach flip-flopping at his tone.

Oh God, no more flip-flopping in that region. That sensation usually indicated her tenuous grasp on control was slipping. And she needed all the control she could muster to face her commander.

Why couldn't he speak to her in her own office? The discussion would be less intimidating for her here. But that was the point. Location was a power issue, she knew. The leader was always the one to sit in the comfortable chair behind the desk in his own office, while the subordinate hovered awkwardly on the guest side.

When the requisite minutes had ticked by, Kylie stood and went to the adjacent building where Mulvany's office was located. Once she was standing across from him he got straight to the point.

"You're no good to me like this," Commander Mulvany said, his expression dead serious.

"Excuse me, sir?"

"You can't keep trudging along like nothing is wrong. You look like you're about to fall apart every time I see you. It's not good for morale."

"But sir, I'm seeing the therapist, and I'm feeling better every day. I think showing up for work is helping me sort through things."

"Off the record, you're screwing up, Thomas. You can't lead in your current state."

Kylie felt as if he'd slid a knife between her ribs. She wanted to double over in pain or curl up on the sofa and cry her eyes out. Of course she didn't dare. Instead she swallowed hard and said, "I'm sorry, sir. I admit I've been distracted by recent events, but I promise you I'll be back to my old self right away."

"I don't want your promises. I want you to take leave. You need R & R time to get over the incident, just like everyone else does."

"Sir, I respectfully disagree. I think I'll go crazy if I don't have any work to occupy me."

"I checked, and you're at use-or-lose level on your accumulated leave. That means you haven't been taking enough vacation, which is a problem under ideal conditions. These are hardly ideal conditions. So I'm going to help you with that problem."

Kylie didn't want to be left alone with her maddening thoughts. She didn't want to go on vacation. She didn't want to appear weak and useless in the eyes of her superiors. How would she ever disprove them of that view if she wasn't reporting for duty everyday?

"Maybe if I take a three-day weekend—"

"No. I want you off for a minimum of two weeks. Even a full month if you'd like. I don't want you back here until you're feeling like your old self again. And I mean it. Either you get better, or you don't come back at all."

She frowned, trying to process what he was saying. It sounded like a threat.

In fact, she was pretty sure it *was* a threat that she'd better shape up or her career was done.

"You have to be a leader of the men and women in

our unit, Lieutenant Commander. Since the shooting, you've displayed none of the qualities of a leader. It's an understandable lapse given the circumstances, but the best thing you can do right now is to get out of here until you are ready to lead again."

And what if she was never ready?

That very real unspoken possibility hung in the air between them.

She might never be ready to lead again.

The realization came to her like a thunderbolt in its clarity. It had been lurking around the edges of her consciousness for days. Her lapse with Drew only made her fear all the more valid. She was acting like anything but a leader—cowering in fear, behaving inappropriately, acting on her passionate instincts instead of her rational intellect.

She swallowed the shame that clogged her throat. She'd had nightmares like this in her early days as an officer, bad dreams of getting called into her superior's office and told she wasn't doing her job well enough, that she wasn't hacking it and she'd better step up or step out.

Having her nightmare come true was so surreal she could hardly think what to do or say next.

"You're looking a little pale," Commander Mulvany said, his brow furrowed. "Do you need to sit down?"

Kylie felt cold and clammy all of a sudden. A wave of nausea hit her, and she saw spots. Without any further warning, her head began to spin, and she had the sensation of falling.

When she opened her eyes again, Commander

Mulvany was hovering over her, his face a mask of concern as he talked into his phone. "She's just opened her eyes," he was saying. "Thomas? Can you hear me?"

"Yes," she said.

"Lie still," he commanded when she tried to sit up.

She was on the floor next to his desk, and she had no idea how much time had elapsed. She'd passed out occasionally over the years—a few times while getting blood drawn, and once or twice when she'd been sick with the flu. But fainting in front of her boss after he told her she was doing a lousy job?

Never happened.

She was losing it. She was really losing it.

Commander Mulvany was right to tell her to get out of here.

"She was only out for maybe a minute," he said into the phone. And then to Kylie, he said, "How are you feeling?"

"I'm okay," she said. "I think I can get up now."

"Yes," he said to the phone. "I think she's going to be all right. Yes, mmm-hmm." He paused, listening. "Okay, thank you."

"Really," she said, pushing up onto her elbows. "It's just my blood pressure is kind of low, and I can pass out easily. I can get up now."

"I'm supposed to get you some orange juice and make you rest for a few minutes." He grasped her elbow and steadied her as she stood, then led her over to the sofa. "You lie here, and I'll be right back."

Kylie lay on the stiff tweed guest sofa, feeling like an utter fool. Not only was she an incompetent leader, but she'd just played the helpless female in front of her superior officer. For a Navy officer, she'd committed an unforgivable act of weakness. Was this the kind of behavior she'd display when under pressure? It couldn't get much worse than that.

As soon as the thought formed in her head, she felt like a shit. It could get a lot worse, if she were one of the victims of the shooting, or one of their family members. She needed to keep her ridiculous career problems in perspective. Her own problems paled in comparison to those of other people.

Soon she heard footsteps coming down the hallway, and her commander reentered the room. He knelt next to her and offered a can of orange juice.

"Drink this," he ordered.

A glance at her boss's tight expression told her exactly how uncomfortable he was playing impromptu nursemaid, and she felt flush all over again with the humiliation of the moment. She would never forgive her body for flaking out on her.

"Thank you," she said after she'd taken a long drink. "I'm feeling much better already."

"I hope you see my point now," he said stiffly. "You need a vacation."

She nodded, unable to choke out an affirmative response. Instead she busied her mouth with another sip while she struggled to regain her composure.

"Yes, sir," she finally said.

"I don't want you to come back here until—and unless—you're ready to perform to your previous standards. Are we understood?"

Kylie nodded. "Absolutely, sir."

And she did understand. She had one chance to change the minds of her commanding officers, to convince them she had the fortitude and qualities demanded by the Navy. And, as her body had proven, she was incapable of performing at that level until she had herself back under control. So mental demons or no, she was on vacation.

7

DREW WOKE UP with a scream caught in his throat. His eyes snapped open. He was trying to cry out, but no sound escaped his mouth. Then his brain caught up with his body and he knew he'd had another nightmare.

He glanced at the clock radio on the nightstand: 7:52 a.m.—past time to get up for PT. Except he didn't have to get up at all today if he didn't want to. He was officially on leave.

He was sweating, even though the room was cool. Rubbing his hand over his damp face, he tried to clear his mind of the horrific images. He'd been dreaming of Kylie at the mercy of a faceless gunman. Drew could only stand by and watch the scene unfold, unable to save her. There were variations on the dream, but inevitably, whenever he slept, he had it.

Logically he knew she could save herself. Kylie certainly wasn't helpless in real life. But for some reason, whenever he saw that nightmare version of Caldwell burst through the door, gun pointed at her, Drew froze…and Kylie paid the price. At first he'd thought his fears were doing a number on him. What if Buckley hadn't distracted Caldwell before he pulled the trigger on Kylie? What if Drew had missed when he leaped at Caldwell? What if Caldwell had gotten control of the gun instead of Drew?

But ever since that night after the bar, he'd wondered if the dreams were a sign that he'd had a thing for her long before he realized. And wasn't that just a load of psychological mumbo jumbo. Man, he'd been seeing the shrink too long.

Still, he cursed his inability to sleep without having nightmares. He climbed out of bed, and fumbled around the bedroom getting dressed to work out. Regardless of whatever crap his mind was sorting through, he needed to be in the top physical condition for the S.E.A.L. test next month. He'd decided to take Justin's advice and spend his leave in Hawaii where he'd add swimming and diving to his regimen.

He downed some water before heading out into the cool morning, then tried to take out his frustrations on the pavement outside.

Running was like meditation for Drew. The rhythmic pounding and breathing put him in a zone where he didn't have to think about anything.

An hour later, he was drenched in sweat and his muscles were tight and hot. Exactly where his body needed to be. Too bad his brain hadn't read the memo about running as meditation. He'd failed to get Kylie off his mind for more than a few minutes at a time. He pushed himself hard through alternating sets of push-ups and sit-ups, then showered and dressed for the day.

By the time he was tying his shoes, he'd made up his mind about what he was going to do. He was going to Kylie's house to tell her she'd be a fool not to explore the feelings that had sparked between them.

He believed in following his heart, and if his heart was crazy, then so be it. Thoughts of her had haunted him, proving that it wasn't the alcohol or the grief that instigated the sex. He had to follow this thing between them, see where it took them and worry about the consequences later. He'd learned from losing his sister and now his colleagues, that life was too short not to go for things he wanted most.

Whatever there was between them, it was powerful, and it deserved to be explored. He wasn't going to settle for less than that.

Also, he had to admit, he was worried about her. The ones who exercised as much discipline and control as Kylie never had the coping skills when life tossed shit their way. She was so close to the edge anything could send her over. It was times like these that friends had to look out for one another. Their unit didn't need a suicide on top of the tragedy that had already occurred.

He drove to her condo, where he'd been once before for a holiday mixer, and was relieved to see her car sitting out front. He parked, got out and went to her door to ring the bell.

When she answered the door, she seemed startled to see him, but quickly recovered. She looked a little less haggard than she had yesterday at work when she'd seemed on the verge of passing out in their staff meeting. Her skin was still pale, and there were dark circles under her eyes that showed evidence of tears.

Drew felt bad for waiting until this morning to

come here. He should have come last night. The truth was, he'd wanted to give her space before launching his let's-hit-the-sheets-again campaign.

"What's wrong?" he asked. As soon as the words left his mouth he knew how dense they sounded. The more accurate question was, what *wasn't* wrong?

She crossed her arms over her chest and hugged herself. "What are you doing here?"

"I was worried about you. And rightfully so, given how awful you look." Oops, definitely not the right thing to say.

"Thanks," she deadpanned. Even so, she stepped back and allowed him in. She didn't invite him beyond the foyer, however, so he leaned against the closed door.

"I mean, I suspect you feel like I do—like you need to get as far from San Diego as you can. I want you to come to Hawaii with me."

Damn it, why had he blurted that out so fast? He'd meant to build up to it, to make a case and show her why she needed to listen to him. Instead, he'd set himself up for more rejection. No way in hell would she be receptive to heading off to the middle of the Pacific with him when it was presented so bluntly. He wasn't even sure he would, either.

"Okay," she said, and he almost didn't hear her.

"What?" He blinked.

"Okay, I'll go." She looked so scared and vulnerable for a moment, he almost didn't recognize her.

"You'll go to Hawaii with me?" he repeated dumbly.

She nodded, and relief flooded his chest. She was

going to do it. She'd be with him and he'd have the opportunity, away from San Diego and her Naval responsibilities, to persuade her to give him—give them—a chance. And if they had something as good as he suspected, then they would have time to work out the logistics of how to be together.

"But…" She seemed to be working something out in her head. "You're going there to train before you take the S.E.A.L. test, right?"

"Right."

"I have a favor to ask, then," she said tentatively.

"Sure, whatever you want."

"I want to train with you."

"You want to train with me?"

"Yes. I know I can't become a S.E.A.L., but I'd like to prove to myself that I can at least keep up with the physical rigors. For personal reasons," she added, looking a little embarrassed.

Drew's first instinct was to protest. He'd already been training for so long, there was no way she could just jump in and keep up with him. She'd slow him down, hold him back, at the very time when he needed to be pushing himself the hardest.

Seeming to read his mind, she said, "I won't slow you down. You can think of me as your trainer, if you want. I'll make sure you're being pushed. Anytime I see that I can't keep up, I'll be your coach rather than your partner."

Which was exactly what he needed right now, he thought, without saying it aloud.

And what Kylie needed right now was to feel as though she had power over her life. She wasn't saying so, but he suspected that was at the root of her request to train with him. He could certainly see the appeal of feeling strong and powerful at a time such as this— and of having something all-consuming to throw herself into, so she could forget.

"Okay," he said. "Let's do it."

"One other thing," she added, looking uncomfortable now. "I would prefer to keep the fact that we're traveling together private. I don't think either of us would benefit from our coworkers knowing about this…."

When she trailed off, Drew knew she was hoping he'd jump in and agree right away. And ordinarily, he would have. He was in the military. He knew what was at stake. But his wounded pride held him back. His reticence made no sense. She was only being practical, yet he hated being something she felt she had to hide.

Still, he knew he was.

Finally, he said, "Okay, sure. My lips are sealed."

"I suppose there's always a chance people will find out anyway. If that happens, we'll just have to handle it as best we can—"

"How would anyone find out if we don't tell them?"

She shrugged. "The Navy's a small world. We could bump into someone we know while we're in Hawaii, or on the way to the airport or in the airport…"

"True," he said. "It's not likely, though."

As much as he wanted to assert his position, force her to get over her worries, he recognized that as his superior, she was the one who was taking the much greater risk in vacationing with him. He was being way too hard on her by sulking about it. She hadn't gotten to her position in the Navy by being foolhardy or fraternizing with her subordinates.

"Thank you," she said. She looked away for a moment before meeting his gaze. "I think this trip will really help me."

"Yeah, me, too."

"When do we leave?"

Not soon enough. "Tomorrow morning," he said, deciding to not push his luck by expressing his real thoughts. He'd have her undivided attention soon enough once they were away from here.

"How are you doing?" she asked. "You look more rested than I feel."

"I've been sleeping, but I have nightmares," he said, then realized his error. He didn't want to tell her his feeble attempts to save her tormented him in every single one.

"About the shooting?"

"Yes," he said vaguely.

"Guess that's normal. The therapist told me they should get better, happening less often eventually. Give it enough time. Who knows? Maybe the change of scenery will make them stop."

Drew nodded. He made a move to leave.

"Just one more thing," she said. "I'm going on this trip with the expectation we will move forward as friends and colleagues, not—"

"Not lovers," he said.

"Right."

"I don't see why we can't," he lied.

In truth, Drew could think of more than a few

reasons why they couldn't be just friends. But there was no point in arguing with her now, when he'd finally gotten her to agree to go away with him.

Kylie crossed her arms over her chest, a gesture that emphasized her vulnerable femininity and made his cock stir in his pants. He didn't want to start thinking sexually about her now, so he forced his gaze not to drop to her soft, round breasts encased in the blue cotton shirt. Breasts that were suddenly familiar and obvious to him now that he knew what lay beneath her shirt.

Instead he studied her expression, which had the same hint of vulnerability he'd sensed a moment ago.

Was this Lieutenant Commander Thomas, standing so stiffly before him, really the same woman he'd made love to so passionately? It seemed almost impossible based on the way she'd behaved before. Before the shooting, when he'd spared a thought to Kylie, she'd seemed more a caricature—the career-driven ice queen—than a real woman. He'd been a fool to assume she was so simple.

He admired the delicate lines of her neck leading up to her strawberry-blond hair. The slightest wisp of a curl had escaped her bun, and it took all his will-power not to reach out and touch it.

As if she sensed his thoughts, her posture and expression changed, and suddenly there was nothing even remotely vulnerable about her.

"Good," she said. "If you e-mail me your travel itinerary, I'll be able to make my arrangements to coincide with yours."

Drew nodded, marveling at how quickly she'd changed. This official Kylie, the businesslike, no-

nonsense one, did a fine job of ridding him of his erection. He straightened and reached for the door. "I'll do that right now," he said and headed for his car.

In the driver's seat, he took a deep breath and sighed. With all of her conditions, his campaign looked grim. Some vacation this would be if she had her way. What had he agreed to? A month of blue balls?

Still, mixed with his trepidation he felt excited when he considered what their time in Hawaii could be like. Warm tropical days, hot tropical nights and an even hotter woman…it could be the most erotic experience of his life. Or it could be hell. If she held out on him for an entire month, not only would his libido be out of control, but also his S.E.A.L. training would be shot to hell.

Funny how Drew had never had trouble getting his way with women, but Kylie was a different story. She had an iron will that came with years of being a military leader. And he couldn't presume his charms would work on her the way they did on other women.

No, he couldn't presume. But he could hope.

What really mattered was that she'd be with him. They'd be away from the Navy's influence, away from the rules that governed their lives—especially hers. With that kind of freedom and his persuasion, the island might work its magic on her, loosen her up. At the very least they'd have the chance they needed to explore the potential between them.

He had to be flexible in his approach to Kylie while maintaining the same determination he brought to his training. And like his dream of becoming a S.E.A.L., he wasn't giving up on Kylie without a fight.

8

KYLIE COLLAPSED on her best friend Sonya's couch. After Drew had left with her promise to accompany him, it was as if something had shifted for Kylie. None of her defense mechanisms worked anymore. There was nowhere she could hide from herself. Instead of feeling weak, however, she was liberated. She'd finally been able to admit she was terrified of sleeping alone. She was exhausted, having endured too many nights of little or no sleep.

Being here in the pleasant surroundings of Sonya's Pottery Barn-addicted apartment, with its splashes of intense color and warm atmosphere, seemed like visiting an alien planet after the past two weeks of insanity. Kylie had known Sonya since their years together at the Naval Academy, where they'd become instant best friends. Instead of sticking with the military as Kylie had, Sonya had put in her minimum commitment and gotten the hell out, as she'd put it, to attend law school as a civilian.

She'd always been too headstrong and rebellious for a life of Naval service, and now she put her willfulness to much better use as a civil rights attorney in her hometown, defending San Diego's poor women and minorities.

Now she sat on the arm of a chair across from Kylie, thumbing through her mail, with her sleek black bob half concealing her honey-colored features.

"So where were you the other night when I called?" Sonya asked. "I worried when you didn't answer, you know. I almost drove over to your place to beat on the door."

"I'm sorry," Kylie said. "I didn't mean to worry you."

"You didn't answer my question." Sonya gave her a pointed look. "Where were you?"

"I was, um, sleeping over with someone."

Her friend's eyes widened. "You? Were sleeping over? With a *guy?*"

"Shut up!" Kylie threw a beaded pillow from the couch at her, but it only hit Sonya's knee and bounced off.

"I'm sorry. I know I'm supposed to be saddened by all that's happened to you—and I am—but this is huge. You actually got *laid?*"

Kylie sighed. Was her personal life really so sad that a one-night stand warranted this reaction? "Yes, I did."

"Who's the lucky stud?"

"No one. Just a guy I met at a bar."

"Wait a minute. Why were you out drinking alone, when I told you to come stay with me?"

"I didn't want to impose," Kylie said weakly.

Which was true. She hadn't wanted to feel like a charity case after the shooting. She'd wanted to prove to herself she was still strong and independent.

And look where that had gotten her.

"I don't believe you slept with some random guy. That's totally unlike you, Kylie. Are you sure you're mentally stable?"

No. Definitely not sure.

Sonya knew her too well, and Kylie was a terrible liar anyway. "Okay, so he wasn't totally random."

Her friend raised one eyebrow. Here was the attorney about to go in for the kill. "Who was he?" she asked, then picked up her teacup from the coffee table and took a sip.

"A coworker."

Sonya choked on her tea, then coughed until she'd cleared her throat. "Excuse me? Did you just say a coworker?"

Kylie rolled her eyes and sank back into the over-stuffed sofa. "Stop grilling me. I'm not on the witness stand."

"I'm going to need the details, you know."

Of course she was. Sonya knew about Kylie's every relationship and sexual exploit—or more accurately in recent years, her lack thereof.

"I've been engaging in some rather unsavory conduct, I'm afraid," Kylie said.

No point in hiding anything from her now. It wasn't as if Sonya would disapprove, anyway. She was Kylie's role model for rule-breaking behavior as an adult.

Maybe *role model* didn't quite fit, since it implied Kylie had followed in her footsteps. No, more like, Kylie lived vicariously through Sonya, who made her own rules and thumbed her nose at everyone else's.

"Fraternizing, eh?"

Kylie cleared her throat. "Yes, um…with a much younger subordinate."

Sonya managed to look impressed. "How much younger?"

"Eight years, give or take a few months. Not that I'm counting," Kylie said. Except that last part was a lie. She'd actually checked Drew's military file after their night together for his exact birth date, just to see how much of a cradle robber she really was. She'd also been reminded by looking at his file that he was waiting for a promotion, due to pin on his new rank of lieutenant, junior grade, next month—which meant, too, that he'd be moving to a new job in a different unit under someone else's command. That still didn't make him anywhere close to being her equal in the Navy, nor did it absolve her of the crime of fraternizing with a subordinate.

"Damn, girl. It's about time you get your groove back, and you might as well do it like Stella did."

"Um, yeah. Except I'm not a gorgeous African-American woman with sass and attitude, and I won't be going to Jamaica. But I will be going to Hawaii… with him…tomorrow."

Sonya looked at Kylie as though her head had sprouted palm trees. "You're serious."

"Yes."

Sonya laughed. "Oh. My. God."

"Could you try not to act so entertained by my downfall?"

"Honey, if you're going to go down in flames, you might as well do it with style."

"I'm not going on this trip as his lover," Kylie

added lamely. "Just as friends. I'm going to help him train for the S.E.A.L. test."

"Of course you are, dear. Keep telling yourself that while you screw his brains out."

"Stop it, this is serious. I can't do that anymore. He works for me. *And* he's too young."

"You might have thought of that before you decided to jet off to Hawaii with him. Besides, you know me well enough to know what I think about the Navy's regulations. Might have been necessary to mandate people's sex lives a million years ago, but not now. And who cares if he's younger? Why should that even matter?"

"It feels opportunistic to me, the same way it is when an older guy preys on a much younger woman. The woman might not feel preyed upon, but that's only because she doesn't have the perspective of the older man's age."

"Are you planning to ruin his reputation? Knock him up and then leave him with a baby to care for all alone?"

"Stop being a smart-ass."

"Kylie, he's an adult. He gets to choose whom he goes to bed with, and he's chosen you. What's so wrong with that?"

Kylie felt a wave of nausea hit her again, but this one was minor compared to what she'd experienced yesterday in her commander's office. She closed her eyes and waited for it to pass.

"Oh, sweetie, I'm sorry for being a brat. I'm really happy for you, you know. It's been far too long since you've let yourself have any fun. I think this trip could be the best possible thing for you right now. Screw what the Navy thinks."

"Easy for you to say."

"Sure it is, because I have your best interests at heart. That's one thing you can't say about the Navy."

Kylie knew she was right. And she was too tired to argue about any of it, anyway.

She'd always admired Sonya's rebelliousness, and it occurred to her that Sonya was the kind of woman Kylie might have become under different circumstances. She'd been living vicariously through her friend for far too long, playing by the rules while relishing every time Sonya broke them. Thanks to getting busy with Drew, Kylie had finally measured up to the strong-woman-on-her-own-terms example Sonya set. It did feel kind of good to finally have something juicy to report about her own adult life for once.

Too bad that juicy bit didn't come close to fitting who she'd become—upwardly mobile Navy officer, straight and narrow, always appropriate.

On the surface, she and Sonya seemed an odd pair of friends, opposite as they appeared. But Kylie knew that she'd have died of boredom if she didn't have Sonya around to remind her that there was more to life than adhering to an external set of rules.

"Oh, stop brooding," Sonya said, interrupting her thoughts. "I didn't mean to insult your first love."

"My first love?"

"The U.S. Armed Forces."

Kylie blinked at that idea. Why did it ring so false to her? She'd been living as if it were true for a long time.

Rather than face the accusation, she decided to change the subject. "Speaking of first loves, what's going on with Angelica? She hasn't been around much lately."

Sonya shrugged, uncharacteristically quiet all of a sudden.

A big part of the reason Sonya had left the Navy so quickly was that she'd realized it was no place for a bisexual woman to thrive. She refused to apologize for her sexuality.

"Trouble in paradise?"

"She's got a job offer in New York City and wants to take it."

"Oh God, Sonya. I'm sorry, that really sucks," Kylie said, though she didn't quite believe herself.

Angelica and Sonya had been caught in a stormy, ridiculously passionate on-and-off relationship for years, both of them a bit too strong-willed to ever relinquish control to anyone else. It didn't make for smooth romantic sailing.

"She's talking about moving next month. I guess I haven't mentioned it because I haven't wanted to believe it's really going to happen. I keep thinking she'll change her mind."

"You know, the way you two get along, you might be better off—"

"I know, I know. You think we're awful for each other. But I've loved her almost my whole adult life. What the hell am I supposed to do if she leaves?"

Whoops. There went Sonya's temper, and she was on the verge of tears now, too.

Kylie felt a surge of sympathy that she was sure showed in her troubled expression. She sighed, then said, "Maybe the distance will make things better between you. You could do the bicoastal thing."

Sonya smirked in spite of herself. "You mean like the bisexual thing?"

"You can be bicoastal bisexuals. You'll start a new trend."

"I don't know…."

"Half the time when you're together, you want to kill her. I know you don't like it when I say this, but I really think you two are in sort of an addictive relationship pattern. Who knows? Maybe the time apart will be the best thing that could happen for you."

"I guess if we were really meant to be, she wouldn't be packing up and moving across country, huh?"

"Did she ask you to come with her?" Kylie dared to ask.

Sonya shot her a look. "No. And I don't want to talk about it anymore. You're going to give me nightmares."

"I'm sorry."

Kylie had watched Sonya's various relationship dramas with bemused interest, always half-fascinated and half-glad not to be caught up in such messy affairs. But for the first time, Kylie could honestly admit that she'd been a bit jealous, too. How much bigger would life be with that kind of passion? That inner wild woman she routinely ignored whispered that Drew could provide the answer to her question.

As if reading her train of thought, Sonya said, "Don't think I haven't noticed how you tried to distract me away from your little cradle-robbing escapade. I expect regular phone and e-mail reports from paradise while you're gone."

"I don't know if I'm going to bring a computer."

"You can dial a phone."

"Okay, okay, I'll report to you my every waking move."

"Good," Sonya said, looking satisfied. "I'm going to need something to take my mind off my woes."

Kylie's throat tightened as she thought about what those reports would contain if she were to relax years of rigid control and let her wild side free. "Don't you think it's kind of…I don't know…shameful to be doing what I did?"

"Sleeping with a guy? No, I don't."

"I mean, a much *younger* guy who is also my *subordinate.*"

Her friend looked unimpressed. "You're going to have to do a lot more than that to get me to use the shameful word. Maybe stab a puppy dog or push an old lady into traffic."

Kylie sighed at the ceiling.

"Seriously, you need to get rid of that faux Puritan streak of yours, my dear. It belongs to your parents, not you."

"I can't help but hear my parents' voices in the back of my head when I do something they'd disapprove of. Doesn't everyone have that problem— everyone besides you, I mean?"

"I think you're getting a double whammy—the God-fearing parents and the moral authority of the Navy. In my opinion, they both need to mind their own damn business and let you live your life as *you* see fit."

Kylie wasn't sure she could trust herself with such a big task. She'd already proven how royally she could screw up her life operating solely with her own judgment.

"I don't know," she muttered noncommittally.

"You're not a teenager anymore. You're a grown woman, and you can make your own decisions about what's right and wrong for you. I wish you'd start living more like you believed that."

Kylie felt something stir inside her, some little twinge that maybe Sonya was onto something. Maybe she was…right? The Navy *and* Kylie's parents did have an inordinate influence on Kylie's behavior. But undoing that was huge and she was too tired to sort it all out right now. "Well," she said, "thank you for believing in me. I appreciate the vote of confidence."

"I've met your parents, remember. I know there are no two people more in need of a good sweaty roll in the hay than Mr. and Mrs. Farmer Thomas."

"Ew. Spare me the image, please."

Sonya laughed. "Do you think they ever do it?"

"Oh my God, stop it." Kylie fought back a yawn. "Discussing my parents' love life is really fascinating and all, but I hope you don't mind if I crash early."

"Sure, whatever you want. You've had a horrible day—hell, a horrible few weeks. I'm glad you called me. This is where you should have been staying all along, you know."

She stood and left the room, returning with a pillow, some sheets and a blanket.

"Up," Sonya said.

Kylie moved out of the way and watched as her friend turned the couch into a makeshift guest bed.

"By the time you get back from Hawaii, I'm sure

you'll be feeling a lot more healed from your ordeal. So I want you to go and have the time of your life, okay?" she said when she turned back to Kylie. "Forget about all the crap that's gone on here."

Kylie nodded. "I'm going to try."

And as she crawled beneath the covers, she halfway believed she'd made the right choice in accompanying Drew to Hawaii. At the very least she was relieved to be getting far, far away from San Diego.

Perhaps sheer madness had convinced her to go to Hawaii with Drew, but she knew that something else was keeping her from changing her mind and backing out. Some complicated set of feelings she had neither the inclination nor the energy to analyze right now.

9

DREW WAS PACKED AND ready to go. He'd reviewed his itinerary, and he'd gotten the house squared away for a long absence. He had to be at the airport in an hour or so. He was just waiting for Justin to show up to pick up Lola and drop off Drew at the airport.

Last night, he'd had a nightmare that Caldwell had broken into his house and killed the cat while he was gone, which was pretty much impossible with Caldwell behind bars, but it had worried him enough that he'd called Justin to ask that the cat stay with him instead of staying here alone. Ridiculous, yeah, but it made him feel better.

He'd originally intended to have his friend simply come here every other day to feed Lola, because she loathed being moved. With the change in plans, he had to strategically hide her carrier until the very last second so that she wouldn't be clued in that a relocation was about to happen, which would prompt her to seek out the hole she'd made in the bottom of the box springs on his bed. Once inside, no one could get to her.

He knelt on his kitchen floor and waited for the cat to climb into his lap. Lola, a self-satisfied gray Himalayan, had been Abby's cat before she died. He and the finicky little fur ball were a wholly unlikely pairing, and he had no idea what he'd do with her on the long deployments that he'd have if he made the S.E.A.L. team. He'd figure out something because he couldn't give her up. No way. She was his connection to Abby and he occasionally felt as though Lola understood him the way Abby had. The rest of the time Lola treated him like the third-class citizen he undoubtedly was in her world.

She stepped gingerly onto his thigh and glared up at him with an expression that contained both affection and contempt. He imagined she was thinking something along the lines of, "I'm wonderful, and you're not, but I will deign to sit on your lap anyway because you are so pathetic."

"Hey, puss. What's happening?"

This was the most embarrassing habit he'd developed since taking the cat. He talked to her. Constantly. She listened fairly well for a cat, and she was good at keeping things private.

"I've gotta go away for a while," he said, and she blinked at him. She'd already figured out from the suitcase next to the door that he was going somewhere, and she had let out a series of yowls after spotting it, to let him know she was none too pleased to be left.

She'd stayed hidden when Kylie had been over a few nights before, because she mostly loathed strangers.

"I'm going on a trip with a woman—the one who came here the other night. And I need to know what the hell to do with her."

The cat purred loudly as he stroked her chin.

"No, I already know to do this kind of stuff," he said, a wry grin playing on his lips. "The problem is I'm pretty sure she doesn't want me stroking her."

But as soon as he said it out loud, he knew it rang false.

"I think she's torn between her duties and her desires. Not that you'd know anything about that, little hedonist that you are."

"Mrrrow."

"Exactly. And I really think I like this woman. Except, well, she's my boss."

Lola eyed him knowingly. If he hadn't known better, he'd have been sure Abby's spirit inhabited this cat. The two shared plenty of the same facial expressions.

"Yeah, yeah, enough with the guilt trip. So do I respect her wishes and not try to encourage a romantic relationship, or do I go for it?"

A knock at the door interrupted their conversation. Lola's chubby body tensed, and she dashed across the kitchen and skidded around the corner, probably heading for her lookout spot under the living-room sofa.

Drew stood and answered the door. Out of all his friends, male and female, Justin was the one who most liked cats and had the best rapport with Lola. In fact, Drew suspected the cat was a little bit smitten with the tan, good-looking blond surfer.

"Hey, man. Sorry I'm a little late," Justin said as he entered the house. "Where's Lola girl?" He let out a realistic sounding yowl, and the cat trotted gingerly into the room.

Justin knelt and extended a hand to pet her.

Drew decided to take advantage of the distraction to get the carrier. A few moments later, he was sneaking up behind the cat with it, and before she knew it, he'd swept her inside and was zipping up the black dufflelike bag that had been designed with little air holes and mesh windows to carry pets.

She let out an angry growl.

"I'm sorry it has to be like this," Drew said, "but you brought it on yourself with that box springs stunt."

When he'd secured the cat, he showed Justin what to feed her and when, then helped him carry the cat, the food and a litter box out to the car. Last, he went inside and grabbed his suitcase.

Once they were all in the car and on their way, Justin said, "So you've got your final training regimen all laid out?"

"Mostly," Drew said vaguely, not wanting to get into the details, such as who his new coach/training partner was.

"And you got my e-mail about my diver friend's contact information?"

"Yep, thanks for that."

"I envy you, man. Wish I was jetting off to the tropics right about now. Any chance you invited some female company along, like I advised you to?"

Drew kept his gaze straight ahead, trying to appear casual. He made it a rule not to lie to his friends. But he'd also promised Kylie he would remain discreet. His promise to her had to come first. "I'm going solo this time," he lied. "I just want to focus on training."

"Hey, I can understand that. Just make sure you

take a break from it sometimes, too. Otherwise you'll burn yourself out before the test."

"My last week there, I'll probably ease up and relax. I'm scheduled to start the official S.E.A.L. test the week after I get back."

"And that's four weeks of hell you'll need to be fully rested for."

Drew nodded, part of him relishing the idea of having his body and mind put to the ultimate endurance test, and part of him terrified of failing. He'd wanted this for so long, and he'd trained so hard, and it was maddening to think that one little slipup or one off day could cost him this dream.

From the backseat, Lola let out a mournful yowl as they went around a corner, and her carrier slid across the seat.

"Do what you need to do to take care of yourself mentally, too," Justin added. "You're going to need to be in top form in every way possible—"

Drew tuned him out. He knew all this, and he could tell his friend was simply keyed up on his behalf. He'd watched a good buddy prepare to take the S.E.A.L. test—and fail at it—so he knew how hard it was to watch a friend endure such an ordeal.

But even knowing the pitfalls, knowing what he had on the line, nothing really seemed like that big an ordeal after the shooting. Nothing seemed nearly quite so important as it had a couple of weeks ago. Sure, he'd be horribly disappointed if he failed to make it on to the S.E.A.L. team. But he was alive, which was more than some of his colleagues could say. Somehow watching comrades die out of combat for no good reason put life in perspective—sort of the way Abby's death had, only in a more brutal, grimmer way.

And that was why he would continue his campaign for Kylie. He understood a little of why her career meant so much to her that she'd avoid anything that might jeopardize it. But he didn't agree with sacrificing potential happiness for a job. In a way, he had to protect her from the stronghold the Navy had on her.

All of a sudden keeping her from losing herself to the uniform, from becoming only Lieutenant Commander Thomas, seemed like the most important thing he could possibly do right now or ever.

Whether she wanted his protection or not, she was going to get it. He felt an overwhelming sense of affection for her already. And the thought of her never again being the sexy, warm woman who'd shared his bed was almost too much for him to bear. Maybe the strength of his feelings was misplaced—the result of having saved her life and now having a vested interest in ensuring she squeezed the most out of that life. And yet, in a way, his feelings seemed entirely appropriate for the heat they'd generated a few nights ago.

"So," Justin said, his tone announcing that he was about to pry. "Are you ever going to tell me what happened between you and Lieutenant Commander Thomas the other night?"

Drew sighed, tearing his gaze away from the view out the passenger window to regard his nosy friend. "No, I'm not."

"You can't hold out on me forever, you know."

"I'm pretty sure I can."

"Must have been a damn good night if you're

being that tight-lipped," Justin said, and Drew tried not to grin.

"Stop it."

"I'm just saying…"

"It's none of your damn business."

"Wasn't I the one who pointed out how hot she is for you?"

"I'm eternally grateful for your meddling, okay? Are you satisfied?"

He wasn't sure why he resisted telling Justin what had happened. He knew Justin could keep his mouth shut. Drew supposed he wanted to protect Kylie's privacy, but it wasn't only that. It was, he realized with a twinge of shame, that he wasn't sure how he felt about going public with the fact that he'd slept with his boss. He didn't want anyone to think the upcoming promotion he was due was in any way a result of doing his superior officer.

And that quickly, he had an inkling of Kylie's concerns. The insight wasn't enough to convince him to change course on the seduction, but it was enough to help him understand where she was coming from.

"Not at all."

"Then you can just use your imagination and make up whatever it is you hope happened."

Justin smirked. "Dude, I don't want to picture you naked."

"Thank God," Drew muttered, relieved that he wasn't going to be pressed for any more details.

Whatever happened behind closed doors between himself and Kylie was to be the subject for his own fantasies and no one else's.

10

KYLIE STEPPED OUT onto the balcony of her hotel room in Honolulu and breathed in the lush, tropical air. It was harder to fill her lungs here, the air was so thick with moisture, but the ocean breeze made up for the humidity. As did this view. Her room looked out toward Waikiki beach and the Pacific Ocean, where the sun was getting low in the sky now. Soon the sunset would be breathtaking.

Her first assignment out of the Naval Academy had been in Hawaii, and she'd always counted herself incredibly fortunate for those two years spent in paradise. Being stationed here had been exactly how she'd pictured her service. It was the polar opposite of the Iowa farm where she'd grown up, and some part of her had needed that extreme change of settings. The Naval Academy in Maryland had wrenched her out of childhood and turned her into an adult, in every sense of the word. Arriving in Hawaii and realizing that she was truly on her own, a world away from the life she'd always known, had introduced her to the potential that existed beyond her upbringing.

So being here now felt both nostalgic and disconcerting. Nostalgic because she loved this place, and loved that time in her life when assigned here, yet disconcerting because she equated Hawaii with momentous change. She wasn't sure she could come here without being transformed by it.

She sat on the chaise longue and stretched out her legs, letting herself relax into the new setting. Maybe what she needed now was a transformation, after all. Maybe she needed to become someone new, someone different. Or maybe she needed to reexamine her priorities. Maybe she'd outgrown her previous life plan and needed a new one that suited her better.

She closed her eyes. Foolish thinking. She had a good life, a solid career…

And it all felt a little hollow, in the face of the shooting.

Before she could contemplate the matter further, she was interrupted by a knock at the door. Kylie crossed her room to the door and opened it. There stood Drew, smiling and holding two open bottles of beer.

"You work fast," she said, stepping aside for him to come in.

"Flying always makes me thirsty," he said. "And it's room service that works fast, not me." He grinned, and her insides did a little flip-flop.

Damn it. She had to stop responding to him that way. He was eight years younger than her. There was no way anything serious could come of their attraction. And she didn't want a fling.

Okay, that wasn't completely true. She did want something, or she wouldn't have come on this trip. And if a fling was all she could have… She'd be lying if she claimed she'd agreed to this trip expecting they could spend weeks together in paradise without *something* happening.

She just wasn't ready to examine her motives too closely…especially with him in her room and the bed right there.

This was the first time they'd seen each other since he'd issued the invitation, and she felt impossibly awkward. She hadn't been able to get a seat on the same flight as him, so they'd arrived separately, but only a half hour apart. She'd called him when she'd gotten into her hotel room, and he'd promised to bring drinks over.

He stopped at the sliding glass doors to admire her view, so she crossed the distance between them and said, "You've got the exact same view, don't you?"

His room was right next door to hers, after all. That, at least, she'd been able to arrange at the last minute even if the proximity seemed to go against her we-can-only-be-friends position.

So what the hell was she doing? Walking into a field of emotional and physical land mines, most likely.

"Yep, but it's a damn good one."

"Definitely worth the elevator ride up sixteen stories," she agreed, then turned and said, "Cheers."

He clinked his beer bottle against hers. "To vacationing in paradise," he said.

Kylie took a long drink of her beer, an ice-cold Dos Equis that went down deliciously smooth. As she swallowed, she realized Drew was staring at her.

"What?" she asked self-consciously.

"It's amazing how different you can be. I mean, your demeanor at work doesn't fit with how you act away from it."

Kylie felt her cheeks warm at his observation, particularly because his expression made it clear which aspect of her he preferred. Then she cursed herself. She was no blushing schoolgirl, and she shouldn't have let a guy's attention affect her that way. It was absurd.

"I don't know what you mean," she said to cover up her embarrassment. "I'm the same person as always."

He shook his head, not buying it. "No, you're different."

"How so?"

"You just seem so much more...womanly, away from work."

Kylie glared at him. "That's sexist bullshit."

"No, it's not. You can't convince me you don't suppress some part of yourself at work."

"Everyone does. It's not a phenomenon relegated to women."

"I didn't mean to suggest it was. But you especially seem to turn off some essential female part of yourself."

Kylie couldn't deny that. She supposed a lot of women did it to survive in male-dominated subcultures.

"In case you haven't noticed, the Navy isn't exactly a bastion of femininity."

"No, and you're probably smart to keep yourself...restrained or whatever."

"I don't ever want to be accused of using my gender to get a promotion."

Drew nodded, appearing thoughtful. "What made you decide to become a Naval officer, anyway?"

"Long story," Kylie said, walking out onto the balcony.

She sat on the chaise again, and Drew followed her, taking a seat on the other chair.

"Great thing about vacation is, we've got nothing but time on our hands."

She sighed. "My dad always talked about his time in the Navy with such pride and wistfulness—completely atypical for him. My parents are God-fearing Iowa farmers. Anyway, he made his service years sound so romantic that I grew up fantasizing about joining the Navy myself. I just pictured it being this idyllic life at sea, traveling to exotic places and all that."

"You must have been a good student, to make it into the academy."

Kylie nodded. "Straight A's. I was a good girl...at least on the surface."

"Do you ever regret it?"

She took another sip of her beer, wanting to avoid such a probing question. A month ago, she'd had few regrets, certainly few she'd acknowledged. But lately they seemed to be crawling out of the woodwork. "Yes, sometimes I do. I think maybe I wasn't cut out to be a leader, since it's partly my fault what happened—"

"No," Drew said sharply. "Don't put that on yourself."

Kylie shook her head, refusing to listen to him. "I could have done things differently. When I think about how I handled Caldwell..."

"You did the best you could at the time, and there's no way his behavior is your fault."

"I think I did treat him unfairly," she blurted. It was her first time admitting it to herself, let alone saying it to anyone else.

"How so?"

She took a long drink to rid herself of the sudden dryness in her throat. "I overreacted. He was accused of rape by a female seaman, and I was in charge of the investigation. In the end, there wasn't enough evidence to be sure what really happened. And…I took her word over his."

"But there was some evidence that he'd raped her," Drew argued.

"It wasn't definitive."

"What made you decide against him?"

"My gut," she said quietly.

"Even if he feels he was treated unfairly, that doesn't justify shooting up an office building full of innocent people."

"I know," Kylie said. "It doesn't. But I'm haunted by the thought that I could have prevented the whole thing."

"So am I. I mean, for different reasons. It's a natural reaction to this kind of thing," he said in an attempt to make her feel better.

It wasn't going to work. Kylie knew her role in the tragedy. And it was maddening that she couldn't turn back the clock, make a different decision in the rape case….

"Stop doing that to yourself," Drew said. "I can see the wheels turning in your head."

She sighed heavily, then drained her bottle.

"I'll try to stop," she said. "Maybe if I drink enough, I'll forget."

"That's a slippery slope we've both already gone down," Drew warned.

"Yeah, and it's only a temporary fix."

"But it sure feels good while it lasts," he said with a wry smile.

Kylie couldn't help but laugh. It had the pleasant effect of easing some of the awkwardness she felt.

"What about you?" she asked to change the subject. "Why'd you join the Navy?"

"Pretty much the same reason you did."

"Didn't I hear somewhere that your dad was a S.E.A.L.?"

"He was, yeah."

"Is that why you want to become one?"

"Hell, no," he said, a sudden harshness in his voice that shocked Kylie.

"*Okay* then. Never mind that question."

He glanced up at her, looking chagrined. "Sorry. I don't have any good feelings about the man."

"Then your reasons for joining the Navy aren't anything like mine. How about giving me the real story?"

The beer, on an empty stomach, had given her a light buzz, and she felt herself loosening up, relaxing as her thoughts and words became less clouded by inhibition.

"What I meant was, I grew up with those same notions in my head of a life in the Navy, traveling across the ocean and all that. Visiting exotic ports, sleeping with exotic women." He grinned.

"Yeah, yeah. That wasn't part of *my* fantasy," she said, and he laughed.

"By the time I was a teenager, I hated my dad for leaving us the way he did. I guess I wanted to prove to myself and to him that I was twice the man he was, that I could walk the same path as him, but do it a hell of a lot more honorably."

"Was he an officer?"

Drew nodded. "Yeah, but he got a dishonorable discharge for conduct unbecoming. Bastard deserved it, I'm sure."

"What did he do?" Kylie dared to ask.

"Had an affair with another officer's wife, but that was long after he left my mother. He was married to his second wife then, and my sister and I hardly ever saw him."

"Well, I'm sure you've already proven yourself. You've got the makings to be a great officer, you know."

Drew looked a little uncomfortable at the compliment. "I guess the real question is whether I can make it past the S.E.A.L. test."

"I'm sure you can," Kylie said, though she knew there was no way to be sure. The test was incredibly strenuous, and one slipup could spell doom for an otherwise perfect candidate.

"Want another beer?" Drew asked, indicating her empty bottle.

"Actually, yeah, I do."

He nodded, then stood and left the balcony, then she heard him opening the door to her room. A few minutes later, he returned carrying a bucket of ice filled with beer. He smiled when he noticed her eyebrows raise. "I ordered a six-pack, but didn't want to seem too presumptuous by showing up with all this beer at once."

He opened a bottle for her and she downed another

long drink. The cold beer tasted heavenly in the warm, tropical air. She should probably eat something before drinking any more, but she never felt hungry these days. Her stomach was tied up in knots half the time.

She looked at Drew, at the way the late afternoon light shone golden on him from the side. It was the kind of light photographers loved, and seeing him now, she wished she had her camera. He was too gorgeous for words, and she could hardly believe she was here with him now. Why did he have to be her subordinate? And why did he have to be so damn tempting? And eight years younger? And not even remotely appropriate for her?

He caught her staring, and curiosity sparked in his eyes. "Can I ask you something?"

"Sure," she said cautiously, "but I can't guarantee I'll answer you."

"Why do you work so hard to ignore the attraction between us?"

"Because it's inappropriate," she said, her cheeks burning again. Yes, she knew a fling was a distinct possibility between them. She was even anticipating it. But that surety and anticipation did not change any of the reasons he was wrong for her.

"Is it really?"

"How could it not be?"

"Pretty soon you won't be my rater anymore. And then what?"

"Then I'll still be eight years older than you."

"So?"

"I've been twenty-six before, Drew. I remember what it's like."

"Everyone is different. You can't claim to know me based on my age."

"No, but I know more about life than you do. I can pretty much guarantee that."

"That's arrogant of you."

"Perhaps," she admitted. "Just as it's arrogant of you to assume you know as much as I do."

"I never said I did."

Kylie wasn't sure what point he was trying to argue. "We both have our careers to consider. I think we'd be setting ourselves up for a painful ending if we entered a romantic relationship."

"I don't think there's any reason to assume that," he said, staring at her defiantly.

Kylie took another drink and felt her resistance slipping. Maybe if they both kept the right perspective about things... If they both understood that this could only be a fling, with no hope of a future together...

She recalled that rush of emotion she'd had after her first night with him, when, for a moment, she'd been sure she was falling in love. That clearly had been her libido, so overjoyed to finally have had sex again, doing the thinking.

If she didn't confuse her libido with her emotions, maybe she could play Mrs. Robinson for a few weeks. Maybe tearing up the sheets would help them heal. Help them forget.

"If anything happens again between us on this trip," she heard herself say. "We have to understand it can't go anywhere."

Drew's expression was unreadable. "What kind of

things might happen?" he finally said, daring her to spell it out.

"You know what I mean."

"Sexual things?"

She stared at him silently, refusing to take his bait.

"What happened to all that talk about inappropriateness?"

"You're being a shit right now."

He took a swig of beer. "You're right. I'm sorry."

"I guess I'm not in any shape to be acting like my most virtuous self at the moment."

"And you think we both might benefit from a little sexual healing, don't you?"

Kylie looked out at the ocean to avoid his gaze. She shrugged, unwilling to admit it out loud.

"It's okay to admit you're human, you know."

"I think I have more than admitted that."

"I don't want to sleep with you if you consider it shameful and wrong," he said, a note of challenge in his voice.

He was backing her into a corner, trying to get exactly what he wanted, rather than accept only what she was willing to offer.

Is that what she felt in her heart? That sleeping with Drew was shameful and wrong?

No.

No, it wasn't. It was the kind of thing her parents might think, or some of her superiors, but it wasn't really what she thought, she had to admit. Otherwise she wouldn't have been able to do it and enjoy it so much.

The real Kylie didn't like living by anyone else's

rules but her own. The person she'd kept buried deep inside for so long made mistakes—sometimes huge ones—but she also lived passionately, fully engaged.

She'd thought she'd banished that part of herself for good. An accidental pregnancy at the age of seventeen had taught that impetuous part of her hard lessons— lessons she never forgot.

But something about the shooting had brought to life long-dead parts of herself. She wanted to be free of her self-imposed constraints and any other constraints that no longer worked for her. She didn't want to feel passive or not in control ever again.

"That's not what I think," she finally said. "What we shared wasn't shameful, nor could it be."

"Then what do you think?"

"I think we're two adults who should be able to do whatever we want in the privacy of our own beds."

And as soon as she said it aloud, she knew it was true. And she knew it was exactly what she intended to do.

11

MIDWAY THROUGH her next beer, Kylie realized she needed to eat something substantial or she was going to have another horrible hangover in the morning. Nursing a sore head and queasy stomach was not how she planned to spend her first day in Hawaii.

She and Drew had continued to hang out on her balcony, talking right through sunset. Because she'd lacked the energy to go out to eat, they'd ordered room service. Drew was at the door of her room paying for it as she lounged, lazily staring up at the night sky.

"Dinner's served," he said a moment later, appearing next to her.

He wheeled the cart to the door of the balcony and began setting their plates on the small drink table between their chairs.

Kylie sat up and felt her belly rumble. She'd ordered a cheeseburger and fries—the perfect accompaniment to beer—and it looked even better than it had sounded on the menu.

But when she looked over at Drew, all thoughts of dinner disappeared and were replaced by more carnal ones of him in her bed. As tempting as it was to tackle him on the spot, another part of her was equally re-

Get FREE MERCHANDISE!

CROSSWORD GAME

Scratch the gold area on this Crossword Game to see what you're getting... *FREE!*

YES! *I WISH TO CLAIM MY FREE MERCHANDISE!*

I understand that my Free Merchandise consists of **TWO FREE BOOKS** and **TWO FREE MYSTERY GIFTS** (gifts are worth about $10) – and everything is mine to keep, with no purchase required, as explained on the back of this card.

351 HDL ESZE   151 HDL ESK3

FIRST NAME   LAST NAME

ADDRESS

APT. #   CITY

STATE/PROV.   ZIP/POSTAL CODE

Order online at:
www.try2free.com

DETACH AND MAIL CARD TODAY!

© 2008 HARLEQUIN ENTERPRISES LIMITED
® and ™ are trademarks owned and used by the trademark owner and/or its licensee.

(HX-B-09/08)

BUSINESS REPLY MAIL
FIRST-CLASS MAIL   PERMIT NO. 717   BUFFALO, NY

POSTAGE WILL BE PAID BY ADDRESSEE

Harlequin Reader Service
3010 WALDEN AVENUE
PO BOX 1867
BUFFALO NY 14240-9952

NO POSTAGE
NECESSARY
IF MAILED
IN THE
UNITED STATES

sistant to the idea. Was he worth ruining her career and her self-respect over?

Certainly not. But hadn't her therapist said to watch out for signs of serious depression, like self-destructive behavior? Was that what this was?

Was she using Drew to self-destruct?

She pushed the thought aside, mostly because she was just buzzed enough not to care too much about consequences right now.

"You're looking awfully serious over a quarter-pound of beef. Is something wrong?"

"Oh." She smiled. "No, nothing."

"I don't believe you," he said, watching her closely.

He had the ability to read people's emotions—or maybe only hers. He wasn't a typical guy that way. He seemed to know exactly what he was feeling at any given time, and appeared unafraid of those feelings. His emotional astuteness was as keen when it came to others. She'd never been with a man who could look at her face and have any inkling what was going on in her mind, and it was a little bit disconcerting.

"Well, to be honest, I was wondering if my attraction to you might be self-destructive behavior. Perhaps a sign of depression."

"Wow, you sure know how to overthink an issue."

"Well, the therapist warned me about uncharacteristic behavior. And I have to say the way I've acted for the past two weeks has been a tad uncharacteristic," she said defensively.

"Beware of listening to therapists too closely. Their job security depends on perpetuating our neuroses."

"That's a pretty cynical way to look at it." Although she did agree with him.

"I don't think most of them set out to intentionally do it. I just think too much navel-gazing and too little living one's life leads to neurotic thoughts and behaviors."

"Am I behaving neurotically?"

"Maybe a little," he said, a teasing smile playing on his lips.

"Okay then, I'm going to shut up now."

She picked up her burger and took a bite, then moaned at the greasy, oozy, delicious mess of it, fairly sure that there was some sort of condiment dripping down her chin.

Drew had ordered a steak, which he was cutting a bite of when she looked at him.

"Don't worry," he said. "I'm not staring at the ketchup on your chin."

"Good." She picked up a fry and used it to catch the extra stuff dripping from her burger. "So, I'm wondering, if you don't recommend thinking too much, then how do you ever grow as a person?"

"By always trying to be a good person," he said, shrugging.

"Don't you have to do a bit of self-reflection sometimes?"

"Sure, but not to the point of torturing myself with it."

"Good thing you're perfect, huh? That must make life so much easier."

"It really does." He grinned and stole one of her fries. "Anything you need to know about life, just ask me. I've got the right answer."

She knew he was joking, but his emotional confidence was undeniably sexy. She supposed it was a big part of what attracted her to him so powerfully.

"I think I have a weakness for people who seem to have all the answers," she said, thinking out loud.

He cocked his head to the side, appearing to give the idea some thought. "Interesting. Do you think maybe that's part of the appeal of the Navy for you? The military's always ready with a set of strict rules to live by."

"Perhaps," Kylie said slowly. "I've always been a little afraid of the results of totally living by my own rules."

"You strike me as a person with good judgment."

She shrugged. "Yeah, but…"

She didn't want to get into any more navel-gazing, especially not after his recent comments on the subject. She had a feeling he was absolutely right.

"But what?"

"But this cheeseburger is far more interesting than my little problems. Want a bite?"

"Sure." He leaned forward as she brought the sandwich to his lips.

He was making a show of being sexy about it, and she couldn't help but laugh.

"What?" he said around a mouthful of burger. "Wasn't that hot enough for you?"

"Smoldering." She pretended to be interested in a French fry, because she was afraid of her feelings showing too much on her face.

She couldn't help but be utterly mesmerized by him.

They chatted as they ate the rest of their dinner, and

Kylie felt herself growing exhausted from the day of travel, the alcohol and the heavy dinner. She yawned noisily, and Drew took that as his cue to leave.

"We should probably get some rest, eh?" he said, stacking their dishes on the room service cart.

"I'm so tired all of a sudden," Kylie said. Despite the exhaustion she had the urge to drag him straight to bed and strip off his clothes.

But…not tonight. If she was going to risk all to have a fling with Drew, she had to do so with a clear head. No more diving into bed with him again thanks to the effects of alcohol. That might be a too-in-control Kylie kind of notion, but it felt right.

Drew's gaze lingered on her as she stood and stretched.

He paused, his hand on the cart that he was about to wheel away. "It was really good talking to you, getting to know you better. I'm glad you came on this trip with me."

"The feelings are mutual. It's been a huge relief already, thinking about something other than…" She didn't want to mention the shooting and ruin the night.

"Yeah. Definitely," he said, rescuing her.

She followed him to the door. "Well. Um…good night."

He looked into her eyes, and she got a little shiver of excitement. It was as if he could undress her with that one little look.

Amazing.

Then he leaned in, and Kylie's breath caught in her throat. Her insides turned warm and oozy at the idea of his kiss, and she closed her eyes. But instead of landing on her mouth, his lips touched her cheek gently, then disappeared.

Kylie opened her eyes and sighed inaudibly. Damn it.

"Good night," he said, then gave her one last sexy appraisal and left the room.

Kylie bit her lip in frustration as she stood alone, staring at the closed door and its instructions for escape routes to take in case of fire or emergency.

He'd given her exactly what her rational mind wanted—a time-out to sort through her thoughts with a sober brain. She should be thanking him, grateful that he hadn't put her in an awkward position by hitting on her and forcing her to turn him down. Or, worse, regret it in the morning. Yes, she should be pleased.

But she wasn't.

Not even close.

WATCHING KYLIE stroll on the beach wearing her swimsuit was enough temptation to drive any man crazy. But particularly the man bent on a slow seduction. The extreme contrast between the bikini of today and the stiff Navy uniform of most days was startling, like an electric shock to Drew's groin. All his reminders to himself not to stare fell on deaf ears.

Surely she felt his hungry gaze on her, could read his dirty thoughts. But she pretended not to notice. In fact, she seemed totally oblivious to his tortured state.

He had to distract himself before he grew an erection big enough to make him the talk of the beach. He'd been thinking of going for a swim, but the moment he saw the surfboard rentals, he got a new idea. "Didn't I hear you like to surf?" he asked Kylie.

She nodded, her gaze following his to the rental booth. "I used to," she said, "but I haven't in a while. I've never quite gotten used to the frigid water off the California coast."

"Then you're in the perfect place to start again."

They were close to the water's edge, and when the next wave came in, she let her feet get wet. "Oh, yeah," she said. "That's more like it."

"Want to go for a surf?"

"God, I'm so out of practice...I haven't gotten wet in a couple of years at least."

"C'mon, it'll be fun."

She looked a little wistful. "This is the beach where I learned to surf, actually," she said. "I was stationed here right out of the academy."

"Really?" Drew hadn't known she'd lived in Hawaii.

He wondered what she'd been like back then. As career-minded and focused as she was now? Probably. Most Naval Academy grads were.

"Yeah, you know, back at the dawn of time," she said wryly.

He chose to ignore her remark. She was only trying to emphasize their age difference, and he wasn't going to bite. If it didn't matter to him, maybe she'd eventually be comfortable with it, too.

"Let's go," he said, taking her by the elbow and guiding her toward the surfboard rental. "It'll be fun, and we'll get a morning workout."

She didn't resist. Thank God, because he couldn't look down at her again right now. His body shouldn't have reacted so strongly to her in that little red bikini, especially since he'd gotten up close and personal with her totally naked body a week ago. But there was something about a healthy, beautiful woman in a swimsuit… Make that woman Kylie, and apparently he had a recipe for his own undoing.

Once they'd gotten their boards, they made their way down the beach to the spot where the waves broke. They were easy, clean, beginner-worthy waves, but Drew didn't mind. It would give Kylie a chance to get her confidence built up, and he could use the practice himself. He wasn't a frequent surfer like Justin was, since the Navy and his training kept him too busy for many time-consuming sports.

They started paddling out. It was still early, but a few surfers were already in the water, and the June air was warm enough to make the cool water refreshing. Drew found himself falling a bit behind so he could watch Kylie's long graceful strokes, the muscles in her shoulders and back flexing. Predictably, his gaze stuck on the unbelievably sweet curve of her ass barely concealed by the bikini and accented by that narrow waist and fabulous legs.

He forced himself to pay attention to the water before he drowned himself or something.

Once they'd gone out past the surf break, they found spots far enough away from the other surfers to keep from getting in each other's path, and they waited.

Kylie looked over at him, squinting her eyes. Her hair was soaked now, slicked back from her face. "You take the first good wave, okay?" she called out.

Drew nodded, and they waited as other surfers took

their turns. Then a new set came in, and Drew saw a perfect wave come along. He started paddling fast, then he was up, his arms out, the force of the wave propelling him forward. It was exhilarating in a way few other things were. He managed to stay up for a respectable amount of time, until the wave broke and he fell into the surf.

By the time he had gotten back on his board and was paddling out again, Kylie had caught another wave from the same set, and she was looking anything but tentative. Her stance on the board suggested she was plenty comfortable, and she appeared like a surf goddess gliding across the ocean.

He watched until the wave dissipated and she took a smooth dive into the water. Perfect execution from the Naval officer. Yet another way she'd managed to surprise him. He could not wait to find out what else she had to hide under that seemingly cold facade.

And if he had any say in the matter, he wouldn't be waiting long. Tonight, he didn't have any intention of spending his time in an empty bed.

12

KYLIE COULD NOT remember the last time she'd had a day packed with so much fun—or a night, for that matter. She wasn't sure when exactly she'd decided to throw caution to the wind, but she had. In a big way.

After the surfing, they'd rested on the beach, gone for lunch, then strolled around town to get themselves oriented. A late afternoon workout had wrapped up their day. Although none of it was particularly eventful, Kylie had been pleasantly surprised to discover that she enjoyed Drew's company.

He was funny, and playful, and smart and quirky. He clearly enjoyed making her laugh as much as she enjoyed laughing at him, which was worth quite a lot when Kylie considered how seldom she laughed in her everyday life.

Even now, as she recalled the joke he'd made about the swordfish, she giggled.

Okay, so there was something to be said for hanging out with a younger guy. He had youthfulness in spades, and not in the annoying way most twenty-somethings she knew did. He wasn't overly cocky and sure of himself while being devoid of wisdom.

Not at all. In fact, he did seem pretty wise for a guy

so young. She'd already sensed that about him from working with him, but she had a much more solid impression of him now. She was taken aback at how much she liked everything she was coming to know about Drew.

Of course, there were the negatives, too. Like…

Um.

There had to be something.

Kylie had just gotten out of the shower and finished drying her hair when she heard a knock at her door. Still wrapped in her towel, she went to the door and peered through the peephole. It was Drew, looking all polished and clean and ready for a night on the town.

Dear God, she was in trouble.

She opened the door and stood aside for him to come in, forgetting for a moment that she wasn't decent. But his appreciative glance down at her towel reminded her.

"Hey, I like what you're wearing tonight," he said.

"Is it too much for dinner, do you think?"

His gaze lingered on her barely concealed body. "Uh-uh," he said slowly.

She could feel the heat in his eyes, warming her wherever he looked.

Yep, she was in big, big trouble.

"There's just one thing," he added, reaching out as if she had a piece of lint on her outfit. "It looks like this would fall off easily."

"Oh?" She watched as his fingertips brushed the edge of the towel, below where she had tucked in the corner.

It felt as if he was moving in slow motion, but she didn't try to stop him as he gave the towel a gentle tug. It fell to the floor, and she stood there naked.

"See what I mean?" he said casually.

"Um, yeah," she said, looking down at herself, not sure what to do.

She could only marvel at the intensity of the raging heat that started low in her belly and caught fire where her legs met. Her nipples tightened at the sudden burst of cool air on her skin.

Drew traced his finger along one breast and around the erect nipple. "Oh, no, you're cold. I'd better help you warm up."

How they got from the doorway to the bed was a blur. Kylie registered only his mouth on her, his hands everywhere she needed them to be. She didn't remember much about how he got his clothes off, but soon he was naked against her, and she was straddling him, kissing him frantically, touching him as if he were the last man on earth.

He'd produced a condom, and slipped it on right before she hovered over his erection and shifted her hips so that he eased inside her, where she was already hot and wet.

She moaned in relief at the sensation, rocking fast and hard to keep him pumping into her, to keep that wild need inside her at bay. This was so good—*he* was so good. How had she gone all day without touching him?

She understood now that she'd been practicing supreme self-control that dissolved in the instant it took a towel to fall.

DREW TRACED his fingertips along the smooth skin of Kylie's belly. He loved the way the glow of the lamplight shone on her skin, the way it highlighted the tiny blond hairs and cast every part of her body in gold. He swept upward, gently tickling the lower half of her breast, then down again, over her belly button, to her hip bone, and along her bikini line to the mound of hair where her thighs met.

His cock stiffened, but he had no intention of rushing things again. Dinner all but forgotten, he figured they could order room service when they got too hungry to go any further. For now, though, he wanted to take things as slowly as possible, to draw out the foreplay until the delicious torture was too much for either of them to bear a second longer. He wanted to know every nuance of her body, and all the ways he could pleasure her best.

She squirmed her hips, urging his fingers lower, but he didn't give in.

"Will you show me how you like to touch yourself?" he said, studying her reaction.

She smirked at him, her cheeks flushing a bit. "No, I will not. Not with you here to do it for me," she said, teasing.

"I'm serious. I want to learn what you like best. Plus it's really hot to watch you get off."

She sighed. "I don't think I can do that."

"For a woman who's so good in bed, you sure do act like a prude sometimes," he said, knowing the taunt would get to her.

She narrowed her eyes at him. "I do not!"

His gaze dared her to protest. Then, unexpectedly,

she slid her hand down to his. Guiding his hand, she put it between her legs, moving his fingers to explore wherever she wanted them. She purred in the back of her throat and shifted her hips to give him easier access.

Drew couldn't complain about her loose interpretation of his request, not when he was so damn aroused.

"It feels really good when you move your fingers like this," she said, guiding his hand in a gentle circular motion.

"Yeah? What else?" He had a good sense of how to please a woman, but he'd had enough experience to know that every woman was unique, and what might have felt like heaven to one wouldn't feel so great to another.

"You've been doing a fine job on your own. I don't know why you think you need my help," she said, but she was clearly getting into the game, her eyes half-lidded and her voice a little breathless as she continued to rub his fingers against her slick, hot flesh.

"Tell me what else you like," he persisted, savoring how beautiful her body looked as she writhed against his touch.

"I like this," she said, moving his fingers again, this time so that they barely brushed against her.

"Yeah?"

"Mmm-hmm."

"How about this?" he said, sliding one finger inside her to find her G-spot, while continuing to rub her clit with his other fingers.

She gasped and closed her eyes. "Yes, that feels… amazing."

Drew leaned in and kissed her neck as he continued to explore with his fingers. Then he whispered into her ear, "Show me something else you like."

For a moment she did nothing. Then she slid one hand up and began rubbing her breast, at first tentatively, but soon without inhibition. She gently pinched her nipple, then tugged at it. "This feels great, especially when I'm about to come."

"Mmm. That's good to know. What else?"

"If you kiss my neck…"

He did so again. "Here?" he whispered.

"Back a little…yeah, right there. It feels almost like an orgasm."

Her body responded with head-to-toe gooseflesh.

Drew trailed his tongue across her neck and up to her earlobe, then nipped at the soft flesh with his teeth. He moved lower, to her collarbone, then her breast, the one she wasn't massaging herself.

"How about this?" he said right before he took her breast into his mouth and gently tugged at the nipple with his teeth.

"Oh!" she gasped again, but arched her back toward him. "Yeah, that's good."

He bit down a little harder, to see where the line was for her between pleasure and pain. She responded with another moan of pleasure. He tried a slightly firmer bite, and she gave a squeal of pain. He made a mental note of this, too. He wanted to know her body as if it were his own.

His own…

He wanted her to be his, pure and simple.

He moved to her other breast, nipping at her fingers, then, when she slid her hand around to the back of his head, he turned his attention to her nipple, sucking and tugging gently with his teeth while he continued to explore between her legs with his hand. By her breathing he could tell she was getting closer to orgasm, so he soon backed off. He knew he could give her an orgasm—or two or three—but this time he wanted to make her wait for it. He wanted to know just how long he could tease her—and himself—before it became too much to bear.

Positioning himself on top of her, he stopped stimulating her and said, "Tell me one of your favorite sexual fantasies."

She blinked in surprise. "Um…"

"It's okay. I don't care if it's weird or innocent or anything in between. I only want to know what really turns you on."

"You clearly turn me on," she said, squirming a bit.

"Besides me."

"I don't know…"

"Yes, you do."

She smiled sheepishly. "Why don't you go first."

"Nope. It was my question. You have to answer it first."

"I don't remember agreeing to those rules."

"I thought I had you at my mercy and could get you to heed my every command."

She made a weak attempt to wriggle out from under him, but her heart clearly wasn't in it. "I suppose you do, but I'm curious to know what sort of leverage you intend to use other than brute force."

"Oh, you know, the sexual kind, since you don't

seem too keen on touching yourself in front of me. If you want to be touched, you'll have to follow my rules."

She narrowed her eyes at him and gave him a swat on his bare ass. "That's pretty cruel, you know."

"Not really. I have your best interests at heart." He rested his head on his hand, emphasizing that he was waiting for her to talk.

After a few silent moments, she cast her gaze up at the ceiling and sighed. "Fine, I'll tell you a fantasy."

_13_

KYLIE HOPED her cheeks weren't flaming red. She'd never talked about sex out loud with a lover before. That probably made her the prude Drew had accused her of being. But she'd never really thought of herself that way. She was pretty uninhibited, and she loved sex, but talking about it…was something entirely new.

No guy had ever asked her exactly how she liked to be pleasured before, and the whole idea of articulating her preferences was revolutionary to her. Was this an uninhibited twentysomething deal where talking was another tool in the foreplay arsenal? Or was this Drew wanting to know everything he could about satisfying a woman, satisfying _her?_ The idea of having her own personally trained lover was tantalizing. Almost enough to entice her to spill a sensual image or two that got her off.

"I've always found something really arousing about water, so my favorite sexual fantasies involve being in water."

"Yeah? Interesting. Go on."

She stared at the shadows on the ceiling cast by the lamplight and continued. "Sometimes, I imagine a romantic night on a boat, just me and a lover, someplace tropical. The water is warm, and we come upon a sea of bioluminescence. We decide to go for a skinny dip, swim around in the glowing light, stroke each other, tease and play in the water. Then we end up on the steps to the boat, our bodies still submerged."

She paused. This was the part where she'd actually have to describe stuff. Sex stuff. Out loud.

"And?" Drew asked.

"And I sit on the steps, and you hold on to the rails and make love to me right there. It's just the water, the boat and the dark, with the glow of the bioluminescence…and the sex, of course."

"So, is the sex slow and sensual, or fast and frenzied, or both?"

"Hmm, I guess both. Depends on my mood when I'm having the fantasy. Sometimes I imagine it raining, too."

"That's a nice start, but I'm going to need more detail."

"Can't we leave anything to the imagination?"

"Nope."

"Of course not," she said wryly. Still there was something wildly liberating about exposing the long-hidden parts of herself, saying things aloud that she'd never spoken before. It made her feel as though she was getting intimate with Drew in a way she never had with any man—in a way that created a deeper bond than she thought it was possible to have.

No. Scratch that. She was getting way too carried away with the romantic thinking. They were simply titillating each other with pillow talk. That was all.

"I'm waiting," Drew said, his gaze half-lidded. He was thoroughly enjoying this, obviously.

If he was going to insist she do detailed and explicit, then she could make him suffer. Get him all hot and bothered then not let him have what he wanted for a while…

When she thought of it like that, the task didn't seem so daunting.

She slid her hand down his side, between their bodies until her fingers brushed his erection. He shifted his weight to the side to give her easier access to him. She gripped him gently, and began exploring him with her fingertips.

"You swim to me underwater and surprise me, slide between my legs, tease me for a while until you know I can't take it anymore."

"How do I tease you?" he said, his voice noticeably tight now.

Kylie resisted a smile of satisfaction.

"At first you use your tongue until you run out of breath and come to the surface. Then you press your erection against me and rub it back and forth, arousing me without entering me. You get me so hot and wet, I beg you to take me right then."

"And do I?"

"No, you keep torturing me. Finally I get fed up and go for the boat, thinking you'll follow, but you stop me and turn me around. You grab on to the boat's stair rails while we're still in the water, and while I brace my arms against the lowest step, you slide inside me and we have passionate, frenzied sex. And it's so good suspended in the water. We can move in ways that are impossible on land."

"Mmm, nice… That wasn't very much detail, though."

"What more do you want to know?"

"How does it feel to have me inside you?"

"It feels like…hmm…like having a full stomach after hunger pains, but better. Like…having an itch scratched in a place you can't reach yourself…" She giggled nervously, hating the way she sounded. "Those are pretty lame descriptions."

"No, not lame. I think these kinds of things are hard to describe because there's nothing else quite like it."

He could be awfully insightful for a twenty-six-year-old. "I suppose you're right."

"Want to know how it feels to be inside of you?"

"Sure."

The corner of his mouth twitched. "Like…um… having an itch scratched in a place I can't reach myself?"

"Except, you can reach it."

"Oh, right."

They both laughed.

"Aren't you going to show me how you like to touch yourself?" she asked. Like everything else about him, she suspected the reality would be so much more intense than her already sizzling mental images of his hands on himself.

"Hell, no. Are you crazy? That's way too embarrassing."

She slapped his arm playfully. "Stop it! I want to see you do it."

"Or what?"

"Or…" She tried to think of some appropriate revenge, but she wasn't likely to withhold anything from him in her current mood. "Or I'll be really annoyed."

"Ooh, big talk."

Kylie tried to keep her expression serious, but she failed. As he rolled onto her and came in close for a kiss, she was nearly overcome with desire and longing and an emotion that wouldn't bear scrutiny if she wanted to keep this fling in I-can-walk-away territory. It was becoming clear that she was in deep, deep trouble, in ways she was only beginning to fathom.

DREW HAD SLIPPED into a meditative state, his mind focused solely on his breathing—in and out, in and out. He and Kylie had been running for a solid hour, first through the jungle and now along the beach. His body had moved beyond the point of pain and was now operating as a machine doing exactly what it was made to do.

Keeping pace beside him, Kylie uttered not a single complaint. When they'd set out, she'd talked, but as the exertion began to tire her, too, they'd slipped into the silent meditation of breathing and running.

Finally they neared the end of the beach where they'd agreed to stop, and they both slowed to a walk. It was only then that the pain of the workout registered. His leg muscles burned, and his lungs ached.

They'd been in Hawaii for five days now—five of the best days of his life. A combination of the company, the setting and the sheer relief from the angst-filled situation they'd left in San Diego had created a wildly heady feeling between them. He knew Kylie was feeling it, too, because he'd never seen her smile and laugh so much.

There was something growing between them that he was happy to nurture, but he could tell Kylie was not.

He banished that thought from his head. No point in ruining a perfectly good time with gloom and doom predictions.

He was happy with the way his training was going. They'd been doing two long workouts daily, and yesterday had been a full day of strenuous hiking. Kylie surprised him with her ability to keep up regardless of the activity. And she was a hell of a coach, pushing him when he lagged and encouraging him when he most needed it.

An afternoon storm was moving in over the ocean, its dark clouds promising rain any minute now. Kylie was looking up at the sky as they walked. She loved the storms—said they reminded her of the epic weather in Iowa that she never really got to experience in California.

They reached a rocky area and stopped, having cooled down sufficiently to do their stretching. He watched Kylie from the corner of his eye, admiring the graceful lines of her body as she stretched her hamstrings, then her calves, then her shoulders.

"What?" she asked when she caught him full-on staring at her.

"I was just thinking that you're beautiful, that's all."

She smiled, but he could tell she was a little uncomfortable with the compliment.

"Yeah, right. Good answer."

"I was also thinking I'd like to strip you naked right

here and take you on the sand like an animal." Not only was his comment true, but also it put her at ease. She seemed more comfortable with the sex than any words or action that suggested emotional attachment.

As if to prove his theory, she burst out laughing.

"I'm serious."

"I know you are. That's why it's funny."

Drew looked around at the rare stretch of deserted beach, and the shelter of the rocks where they stood. "We probably wouldn't even get caught."

"I'm not sure I want to test that theory."

"There goes that conservative streak of yours again," he said, half disappointed at her reluctance to be daring, and half wanting to get to the heart of why she was afraid. This wasn't the first time he'd butted up against her fear, but it was the first time he wanted to really push the issue.

A hurt expression crossed her face before she recovered and presented her usual cool mask of detachment to him. Thanks to this time together at least now he knew it *was* only a mask, and not an accurate representation of her real feelings.

She sank onto the sand, her legs out in front of herself, and reached for her toes without commenting.

A wave of frustration hit Drew. He wasn't going to let her avoid the topic.

"Seriously, Kylie. Why does it seem like there are two sides of you that are so different?"

She sighed. "I don't know what you're talking about. Lots of people wouldn't want to have sex in a public place. I don't think that makes me emotionally flawed."

"It's not just that. It's the way you present yourself

to the world. At work, you're an ice queen, but since we've been together this past week, you've been so warm and passionate and real. But when I least expect it, the ice queen comes back."

"Like now?" she said sarcastically.

"Yes, exactly."

"Your male ego won't let you accept even a minor rejection, so you have to blame it on me being frigid, right?"

Drew winced at the accusation. "That's not fair, and it's not true. This has nothing to do with my ego. And I wouldn't classify this as you rejecting me at all."

"Then what's the problem?"

He knelt in front of her and took her hands in his, forcing her to look at him. "I just want to understand. *Really* understand."

"Understand what?"

"You."

She blinked at that, clearly unsure what to say.

"Why?" she finally asked.

"Because I'm interested. You're someone I care about. How could I not want to understand you?"

She took a deep breath and drew her legs up into a crisscross position, then rested her elbows on her knees. She looked out at the approaching storm.

Fat drops of rain began to fall on them. After a few seconds, the drops morphed into buckets, and they were forced to seek shelter. A rocky outcropping nearby formed a sort of half cave, and they dashed for it. By the time they were beneath the cover, they were drenched. But the rain went a long way toward cooling him after that hard run.

Kylie sat on the sand to watch the rain fall over the ocean, and Drew sat beside her, patiently waiting for her to speak.

When it seemed like she would remain silent forever, Kylie said, "I guess I should explain. This happened to me a long time ago. I never talk about it, but my whole life changed then. And I changed."

"What was it?"

"I was seventeen, and I was known as the town wild child. I'd always been a good student, and on the surface I followed the rules well enough to keep my parents happy and get into a good college when it was time. But I had this part of myself that desperately needed to rebel."

"And that's the part of you I've been getting glimpses of, right?"

She shrugged. "I guess so. It's been a long time since I've let myself even bend a rule, so maybe you're right."

"What did you do to rebel then?"

"I snuck out and partied. I drank, I experimented with drugs…and I had lots of casual sex. My parents would have been horrified if they'd known the half of it."

"They never found out?"

She shook her head. "I was an expert at sneaking. And because I kept up my grades and went to church and did what they asked, it never occurred to them that I wasn't what I seemed. They trusted me so never checked on me after I went to bed. I'd climb out my window and meet up with my friends. They were older and didn't go to my high school, so the chances of my rebel life intruding on my daily life were pretty remote. You know what's funny? I was doing all this crazy stuff and no one bothered to look past the good-girl persona to see that I was heading for a whole lot of nothing good. People only see what they want to see."

"So what changed? Did you get caught?"

"No. I got pregnant. The game was up."

"Oh, wow. That must have been rough."

"It was absolutely terrifying. One broken condom showed me exactly what a shallow, reckless brat I was. I'd gotten accepted into the Naval Academy and suddenly I wasn't so clever for juggling this double life and pulling a fast one on everyone. Instead my stupidity threatened my future—I couldn't go to the academy with a kid in tow. Worse, when I told my parents, they were devastated. I don't think I'll ever forget the look on their faces—like I was a deceitful stranger who'd stolen their precious daughter."

"So what happened to the baby?"

"I knew I wasn't ready to raise a child, especially not alone. I didn't even really know the father. He was just some guy…"

Her voice trailed off, and Drew felt a pang of sympathy for the scared girl she'd been. It could have just as easily been him or any of his friends who'd made such a mistake.

She continued. "My parents wanted me to have an abortion, even though they'd always been opposed to it. They were so afraid of me messing up my life. They were so desperate to have their plans for me work out, as if by maintaining my grade point average then going to the academy, we'd be able to put this unfortunate incident behind us and I'd be the daughter they'd thought I was. There were times when I was convinced their plans for me meant more to them than I did." She sighed. "Despite their pressure and expectations I decided to go ahead and have the baby, then give it up for adoption."

"And did you?"

She swallowed hard and looked away. "I had a miscarriage when I was almost three months pregnant. I guess everyone considered it a blessing of sorts. But I didn't. I just felt so sad."

Drew wanted to comfort her, but words escaped him. He really couldn't begin to imagine how she'd felt.

"It was impossible to explain to anyone why. I got really depressed after that—stopped talking to my friends, stopped going out. I just went through the motions of my final semester of high school in a daze."

"You'd gone through a major trauma. It makes sense that you were depressed."

"Everyone around me was so relieved. My parents kept saying it was God's will, that I was given a second chance—stuff like that. Yet it all felt so wrong and so sad. No one seemed to care that a baby—my baby—had died."

"Yeah, they were probably too caught up in worrying about your future to look at it that way, huh?"

"I guess." She paused, biting her lip as she watched the rain. "It's so strange to talk about it now, after all these years. I really haven't talked about it to anyone."

"Ever?"

"Ever."

"I'm honored that you're sharing it with me," he said, feeling lame even before the words exited his mouth. They weren't adequate to express how he really felt. "How did you get past it so you could go on to the academy?"

"I don't know. If anything, the academy did it. That first year was so grueling, and such a different world. I was so physically and mentally exhausted that I could only think about surviving each day. It kind of helped me forget."

"I guess that's the intent. That first year breaks down who you were and turns you into someone new." He'd never attended a service academy, but he'd heard the stories of how brutal they were.

"Right. In a way that's what I needed."

"I've heard one way to cure depression is to get your mind totally engrossed in something new."

Kylie nodded. "I never thought of it that way, but yeah, I suppose that's what cured me."

"Except, everyone needs someone to talk to about this kind of thing. Holding it in for all these years is a pretty big burden."

She looked at him, and he was surprised to see what appeared to be an expression of gratitude in her eyes. "Especially around my parents. I think it's always bothered me that the pregnancy and miscarriage have become a taboo subject no one ever mentions. We pretend that part of my life didn't happen."

"You don't have to pretend, though. You can't control what your parents do or say. If they're ashamed or embarrassed, that's on them, not you. You have to make your own peace with your choices. Past and present."

Outside, the rain fell heavier, and the waves crashed closer and closer to the rocks where they sat. Drew was pretty sure the tide wouldn't reach them, but he kept an eye on its movement just to be safe.

"You're right," she said. "It's odd how we can get trapped into the roles our families set out for us. We never think of questioning them."

"I don't have that same pressure since it was mostly me and my sister trying to survive. There wasn't much in the way of parental expectations."

"I don't know why I let mine become so influential. It's like all that rebellion as a teenager never took place. I've spent my whole life since then trying to be the perfect daughter, trying to regain their trust and redeem myself."

"Guilt can do that."

She nodded.

"Maybe you need to forgive yourself."

"I think what I really want," she said, her voice sounding uncharacteristically shaky, "is for my parents to forgive me."

He reached out and put a hand on her thigh. He wanted to pull her close and hold her, but he knew she'd resist. He sensed she had more to say. "They've never given you that?"

"Not overtly, no. Like I said, they act as though those months didn't happen. But they're cautious around me, as if they're braced for the next big revelation about my true character, the next disappointment."

"Maybe you should tell them how you feel."

She laughed out loud then, a bitter, harsh laugh. "God, that would blow their minds. We don't talk about how we really feel in my family. We stay tight-lipped and pretend everything's okay, all the time."

"Do you think some part of you has always been rebelling against that?"

"I don't know if it's that complicated. I was a kid, and I wanted to have fun. I felt a lot of pressure, being the only child, to be the perfect daughter. So I blew off steam—albeit in a self-destructive way."

"It makes sense. They were probably way too strict, right?"

"Yeah. I don't know why, but I've always felt like their way was right and anything else was wrong. Maybe because their way was so close to what I heard in church every Sunday."

Drew thought of how she had always seemed so controlled, so exacting, and it made a hell of a lot more sense now. "You don't have to follow all the rules all the time to be a good person."

She shook her head. "I'm halfway through my thirties and haven't figured that out yet?"

"You've been doing a pretty good job of doing your own thing lately."

"Yeah," she said quietly. "I suppose I have."

"Maybe you just need to relax and go with it."

Thunder boomed overhead, and a warm breeze whipped at them. Kylie pushed her hair out of her eyes as they watched the storm bending the palm trees outside. Drew understood her a lot better now. Her duality, the way control and uninhibitedness seemed to battle inside her. She was even more attractive to him now that he knew how she'd come to be the woman she was.

A coy smile played on her lips then. "You think?"

She slid across the sand closer to him, taking his hand and moving it up her thigh. Then she straddled his lap and dipped her head to kiss him.

Right before her lips met his, she cupped his half-erect cock and whispered, "Still up for action?"

14

KYLIE WASN'T SURE what had gotten into her. She normally didn't consider talking about her parents or her checkered past a prelude to sex, but at the moment, she couldn't think of anything she'd rather do than get Drew naked right here on the beach. The rain had chased away the last of the beachcombers and swimmers, so whatever bit of modesty had been holding her back was gone.

Thunder rumbled overhead as she tugged off her top. Drew stared at her, looking a little stunned.

"I'm glad you took my advice so quickly," he said when his gaze dropped to her now-bare chest.

He slid his hands up her belly and cupped her damp breasts in his palms. Between her legs, she could feel his erection growing harder.

"I'm all sweaty," he said. "Want to swim first?"

"I want you inside me," she said, her voice husky with desire. She nipped at his earlobe, then his neck, kicking off a wave of sensation in him.

He let out a ragged breath and grasped her hips, pressing himself harder against her. "You'll have me inside you soon enough."

Then he set her aside and stood, grabbing her hand and pulling her up.

"You're going to make me wait now?"

He smiled a half smile and shrugged. "C'mon, let's take a dip in the rain."

Kylie loved the feel of the rain against her skin, so didn't argue further. She peered out around the rocks to make sure the coast was clear, then stripped off her shoes, socks and bottoms. "This is the part where I admit I've never been skinny-dipping."

"Not even as a teenager?"

"Nope."

"You've been missing out."

He was naked now, and he took her hand to sprint across the sand into the crashing surf. The wind and rain on her skin was one of the most luxurious feelings she'd ever experienced, and she squealed with the delight of it.

When they reached the surf, Kylie waded in without hesitation, Drew just ahead of her. Once he was waist deep, he turned and pulled her to him, lifting her in the water so that she was a little deeper than him, her bare chest concealed by his. The waves lapping at them concealed that they were both naked.

"There, you're safe now," he murmured. "No one can see you."

But safety was the last thing on her mind. She felt carefree, intoxicated by the sudden freedom she felt— a freedom that was both literal and figurative.

She wrapped her arms around Drew's shoulders and her legs around his thighs before kissing him for all she was worth. There was no worrying about anything at the moment. She wanted nothing more than the sensations of his body against hers, of the rain and wind and ocean on her skin. She wanted to absorb it all so that she'd never forget the luxury of it.

His tongue lapped hungrily at hers. From the hardness of his erection nudging her, she knew that he wanted her as badly as she wanted him. Only then did she remember that he wasn't wearing a condom.

"I don't have any protection," she said.

"Neither do I."

She felt a moment of panic. She took birth control pills—just in case—but she'd always considered condoms a necessary precaution.

"I've been tested recently, and I'm clean," he said.

"Me, too," she said, but still that deep-seated phobia held her back.

"Are you worried about getting pregnant even on the pill?" Once again he astounded her with his perceptiveness.

"I know it's safe. I'm just…" She shrugged, at a loss to articulate such an irrational fear.

"Hey, I get it. We don't have to do anything, okay?"

His willingness to concede to her neuroses put it in sharp focus. She was safe with him. "No," she said firmly.

This was her chance to prove she could accept the risks inherent in living a full, rich life. She was going to take it. She needed to prove to herself that she could.

He looked at her with those enigmatic blue eyes, and she couldn't help but melt under the power of his gaze.

"I want to do this," she said, to make sure he understood, and she shifted her hips then to allow him easier entry.

He positioned himself at her opening and slid inside, just as a wave broke nearby and the foaming surf washed past them. She moaned at the pleasure of it, and rocked her hips in time with his, accepting him as deeply inside as he could go.

Her clit rubbed against his abdomen, causing her enough stimulation that she felt on the edge of orgasm after only minutes. He pumped into her slowly at first, but his thrusts came faster until Kylie could only hold on for the ride.

He was panting against her neck, moaning softly under his breath, as she felt herself start to go over the edge. She cried out at the suddenness of it. The startling intensity overtook her as another crack of thunder sounded overhead.

Kylie cried out, gasping as the waves inside her body became so much more intense than those surrounding them. She realized, as the orgasm passed its peak and the waves of pleasure slowed, that she was reacting as much to the sensation of his bare, unsheathed skin inside her as she was to any of the other stimuli.

Having him bare inside her was physically intimate in a way nothing else they had done together was. And she understood, in her extreme caution, yet another pleasure she'd been denying herself all these years.

Drew's thrusting quickened, then faltered as he reached his own climax. He held her so tightly she almost yelped.

He gave a final thrust and groaned against her ear, then reclaimed her mouth in another hungry kiss as his breathing calmed.

They ended the kiss, yet remained quiet, as if unwilling to break their connection. The moment stretched, until she started to feel too vulnerable and exposed. With his usual insight Drew changed the mood by licking a raindrop from Kylie's nose, then he smiled at her and sighed heavily.

"Wow," he said. "You don't mess around."

"Me? Far as I could tell, it took two of us to do that."

"I was just along for the ride, babe."

"You were leading the cavalry." She backed up and splashed him, which was ridiculous as an assault since they were already soaked.

He laughed and pulled her closer. "What do you say we get out of here before we get struck by lightning or washed away in the downpour?"

"We've been safe so far," she said, then threw herself into the surf to float.

"We've been pressing our luck," he said, but his gaze was fixed on her chest rising above the surface of the water.

He was probably right. Yet Kylie was still in the process of proving to herself that she could live on her own terms. It was all such a new, thrilling, exhilarating idea to her. She felt like she needed to stick with it to make it real.

She began a lazy back crawl that took her farther from shore, her body gliding easily over the surface of the water as waves bobbed her up and down.

Drew dove in and swam beside her. "How far you going out?"

"I dunno."

"Is it safe to swim after sex?" he asked with a wry grin.

"Hmm, good point. We might get leg cramps or something, huh?"

"Personally, I might collapse from exhaustion."

"So go back to the beach. I'll be there soon."

"I'm not leaving you," he said.

"I'm a strong swimmer."

"I know you are, but I'm still not leaving you."

A loud clap of thunder sounded again overhead—this one stronger than any of the previous ones. Okay, there was a fine line between being a risk-taker and being stupid. She rolled onto her belly and started swimming toward shore. Drew followed.

As they reached the sand, she ran toward the rocks and started getting dressed, but she was so wet, getting back into her clothes was no small feat.

"How about we run for the car?" Drew asked. "There are some towels in the trunk."

"You mean, naked?"

"Sure, why not?"

She glanced around, reminding herself about the whole living in the moment thing she'd been determined to do just minutes ago. She could handle this. No big deal…

She gathered her things then bolted across the beach to where they'd parked the rental car on the side of the road earlier. Drew quickly caught up to her.

This was ridiculous. They were two grown adults, totally naked in broad daylight running through a thunderstorm. They could get arrested, or electrocuted, or photographed by weirdoes or all of the above.

She started laughing and couldn't stop. Soon she was laughing so hard she had to slow to a walk.

"What?" Drew asked, smiling at her laughter.

"Us. We look ridiculous," she said between laughs as she held her aching stomach.

"No, we just look naked. From my angle you're looking pretty damn hot. *Ridiculous* isn't a word that comes to mind at all."

Kylie tried to catch her breath, ducking as a car drove by. No, she really didn't care. This would probably be a moment she'd look back on in her old age and see as one of the highlights of her life. If she couldn't enjoy it fully now, then she was a sorry excuse for a human being.

And with that thought, she relaxed. Another car went by, and she didn't care this time. She grabbed Drew's hand and pulled him to her, then kissed him long and hard. When she broke the kiss, he looked both pleased and stunned.

"Where'd that come from?"

"From me, to say thank you."

"For what?"

"For this." She kept walking, leaving him to catch up as he contemplated what she meant.

"Sex on the beach? Anytime, babe. I'm your man."

They reached the road, and dashed for the car while the coast was clear. A few minutes later, they were sitting in the shelter of the front seats, toweling off and struggling to get into their clothes.

Kylie succeeded at putting on her top and shorts, but she didn't bother with her shoes.

"Have you ever had a moment in your life when everything is suddenly clear to you, when you feel like you're right where you're supposed to be, doing exactly what you're supposed to be doing?"

Drew gave the matter some thought. "I think I felt that way the first time I went diving."

Drunk with her own happiness, she felt as though she could say anything. "That's how I feel right now."

It was true. She couldn't remember the last time she'd felt more like herself than she did right here and now—and she never wanted to lose this feeling.

15

AFTER ALMOST TWO weeks in Hawaii, it amazed Kylie how easily she forgot about her life in San Diego. Those fantasies about Drew she'd entertained had seemed so far beyond her reality a few weeks ago. Now she'd not only acted them out, but also she'd discovered how much better reality could be than fantasy—how much more detailed and satisfying. If she weren't so blissed out, she'd be concerned about her lack of imagination and creativity.

She tried her best to avoid thinking about how soon her visit out of time with Drew would come to an end. But every once in a while, she'd get a pang of fear when she thought about how tenuous her grip on this existence was.

Such as right now. She and Drew were strolling along the marina, a flaming pink and orange sunset on the horizon. It was romantic and dreamlike and she hated the thought that these moments were soon going to end.

"What are we doing here?" she asked to distract herself from the nagging worry.

"It's a surprise."

"Well, let me guess…it has something to do with a boat, since we're surrounded by them right now."

"I'm not telling."

He was acting like a little boy on his way to the candy store, and Kylie couldn't help but be charmed by his excitement. He'd been mysteriously planning something all day that he wouldn't share. She suspected it had something to do with the boat fantasy she'd described to him when they first arrived in Hawaii.

She blushed at the thought of acting out the fantasy—especially such an elaborate one—even while she was tantalized by the possibility. If her imagination proved to be as lacking in creating a fantasy as it had with the others, she was in for a scorching experience.

They reached a small yacht, and Kylie saw a candlelit dinner set up on the deck. She laughed. "Are you serious?"

Drew smiled, took her hand and led her across the gangplank to the deck.

"I'm serious about being hungry," he said. "Hope you like oysters."

"I love them. Who set all this up?"

"It's magic. I snapped my fingers, and—"

"Oh, stop it."

"I can't ruin my mystique by telling you the inner workings of my plan."

"Of course not. Sorry I asked."

He pulled out a chair for her, and she sat.

"I thought we'd better eat before leaving the dock, if that sounds good to you."

"Absolutely." Kylie surveyed the food on the table and could hardly believe how good it looked—a delicate red beet salad with goat cheese, orange slices and walnuts, baby asparagus, fresh French bread and a selection of oysters on the half shell. A bottle of chilled white wine had already been opened and poured, probably only minutes ago.

She looked at Drew and shook her head. "I'm amazed."

"Good." He picked up his glass of wine and toasted. "To fantasies," he said.

She smiled shyly and touched her glass against his, then looked out at the water and shook her head at how ridiculously perfect it all was—better than her fantasies.

Growing up in landlocked Iowa hadn't afforded Kylie opportunities to experience life aboard a boat. The Navy had changed all that for her; however, no matter how challenging serving on a military vessel got, she'd never quite gotten over her romantic ideas about the seafaring life. Blending her once-in-a-lifetime fling and her love affair with all things nautical was almost too perfect to be believed.

The boat rocked gently on the water, and Kylie looked out at the open ocean as she imagined what was on the other side. Japan, China, all of Asia.

"What are you thinking?" Drew asked.

"I was just imagining faraway ports of call."

"Have you ever been to Asia?"

"On deployments. And I got to travel around Thailand for a while after one tour."

They chatted about traveling as they ate. Drew hadn't been to many ports of call yet, but he would soon enough. Kylie had a feeling he was going to make the S.E.A.L. team. The more time she spent with him, the more she recognized that he had the drive and the focus to do it.

By the time they finished dinner, she had a slight buzz from the wine. A waiter appeared from the cabin bearing dessert. He lit a plate of bananas on fire, then made quick work of serving them over ice cream.

"Wow," Kylie said. "Bananas Foster?"

Drew smiled. "It's a little showy, I know. Too much?"

"Not at all. I'm just amazed—it's my favorite dessert."

"Really?" He looked pleased with himself.

"Really." It was one more absurdly perfect detail to emphasize that this was a whole state of fantasy they existed in.

Kylie tried to ignore the uneasy feeling in her belly that this was too good to be true. She could live this way forever, she knew, pretending sunset dinners aboard yachts were real. But they weren't. She was still Drew's commander, and this affair was still forbidden. There were still two disparate lives they'd left behind in San Diego.

After the waiter had served them, then disappeared, Drew leaned across the table and took her hand.

"What's wrong?"

"I'm sorry, it's nothing. This is all really perfect. Thank you."

She felt like a total shit for feeling anything but thrilled at all the effort he'd put into the evening.

"No, don't lie to me. I saw that expression that just crossed your face."

What could she say? That she was too caught up in

her Mrs. Robinson role and had forgotten that it was just that—an act?

No.

Not now, anyway. She owed him the enjoyment of this night he'd planned for her.

"You're too damn intuitive for your own good," she said, hoping to distract him.

"Were you thinking about San Diego? What happened?"

Kylie nodded and cast her gaze down at her dessert. That was close enough to the truth. "Yeah. I guess I had a moment of feeling guilty that we're here having so much fun, and other people…aren't. You know?"

"Yeah, I know. It hits me sometimes, too, at the oddest times."

An awkwardness descended. Kylie didn't want to ruin this night, especially after Drew had gone to so much effort for her. She picked up her spoon and forced herself to take a bite. The flavor was exquisite enough that there was no way not to enjoy it.

"This is amazing," she said.

Drew was still watching her. "This trip really is helping us heal, you know," he finally said.

"I know. I can feel it. Sometimes I don't believe I'm entitled to be happy so fast."

"We have to hold on to happiness whenever we can. There's no rule that says we have to suffer constantly to mourn the loss of people we care about."

"I guess you'd know about that better than I."

"One hard lesson I learned was that it's impossible to go on with your life and stay sad. We're not really honoring the dead when we do that."

"No, I suppose we're not," Kylie said quietly, stirring the bananas and ice cream.

"The only way to honor the dead is by living life to its fullest. As cliché as it sounds, life is a gift. It's gone too fast not to cherish every second of it."

Kylie shifted uncomfortably in her seat at the raw, unvarnished sentiment behind his words. Cliché, yes. But the thing about clichés was they often revealed the most basic truths about life—the things everyone experienced.

"You're right," she said. "Thank you. I need to learn not to feel guilty about being happy."

"Yes, you do." He went quiet for a moment, then leaned in close and added, "Because I've got more fun planned."

She couldn't help but smile at his leering expression. "I don't know. We might have trouble finding bioluminescence tonight."

"That's okay because I brought the next best thing," he said, leaning over and retrieving a box from beneath the table.

"What is it?"

"Glow sticks."

Kylie bit her lip when he pulled out a little plastic tube of green liquid. "Perfect," she said.

He set the box aside and dug into his dessert.

His thoughtfulness humbled her. When was the last time a man had taken such care to ensure she was happy, her wishes fulfilled? When was the last time she'd *allowed* a man to do so? That Drew had listened to her then recreated her wishes down to the last detail of her favorite dessert and glow sticks overwhelmed her. What a barren wasteland her emotions had been.

How many wonderful experiences had she cut herself off from while trying to keep herself under control? Drew had given her a bigger gift than he'd ever know.

She reached across the table to clasp his hand. "Thank you," she whispered around the tightness in her throat. "Thank you for this trip, for this night…for the romance. It's been far too long since I've experienced something like this."

"Yeah?" He turned over his hand so their palms touched and their fingers entwined. "Why is that?"

She shrugged. "The usual. Too caught up in my career."

"That sounds like an excuse."

"Maybe it is. I don't know."

"When's the last time you had a serious relationship?"

"Define serious."

"You know. In love with someone."

"In love?" she said, stalling. There had been only one time when she'd thought she was in love—the first time she slept with Drew.

"Yeah, head over heels, crazy in love."

"I…um…haven't been."

"Ever?" He looked stunned.

"Ever."

"How could that be?"

"Maybe my definition of love is too strict. Maybe I've played it safe and never let anyone get close."

"Haven't you ever dated anyone long-term?"

"Oh, sure. I've had a couple of relationships that lasted a year or two. But even at the time I knew I wasn't fully engaged. It was real easy to let the next deployment or the next promotion be an excuse to walk away."

"I don't get that. Why'd you stick around if you weren't into it?"

"Companionship?"

"Did they fall in love with you?"

Kylie winced. "They claimed to."

Drew wore a disbelieving expression as he withdrew his hand. "So you strung along these saps until, what? You got bored? Or until you got promoted and could cuddle up to your new rank. Man, that is cold."

The warmth and affection she'd been nurturing from Drew abruptly ceased as he continued to stare at her. "That's harsh. Those relationships have nothing to do with you."

"Don't you get it? They have everything to do with me—with us. You hold yourself apart, never letting yourself commit. Meanwhile the guy, the poor sap, is turning himself inside out trying to get your attention. But there's no point, is there? Because no man can compete with the mighty Navy for you esteem, can he?"

He stood and began to pace. "God, I've been such an idiot. Here I've been busting my ass to show you that we could have something amazing together and you're just looking for exit."

Panicked, Kylie couldn't speak. Not only was his attack out of left field, but also the real possibility she could lose him—had already lost him—froze her in place.

"Well, aren't you going to say something?" He paused, then turned his back on her. "Of course you're not."

Seeing those broad shoulders averted spurred her into action. She rose and approached him, hesitating only a moment before wrapping her arms around him and resting her cheek on his rigid back. "Drew, I swear it's different with you. I have no proof of that. I can only tell you I feel things for you I've never felt for anyone. You mean more to me than the Navy, than my job, and that scares the crap out of me."

Something about her clumsy apology seemed to have an impact on him because his muscles relaxed as he turned to embrace her. The relief flooding her system made her knees weaken.

"I'm sorry, Kylie. I shouldn't have said that shit to you. Guess I freaked a little at the thought I might not be important to you."

"You are, Drew. I just don't know how—"

"Let's not worry about the hows tonight, okay? We'll figure it out. In the meantime, we've got a moonlight cruise and some glow sticks that need our attention." He said the last with a leer that made her laugh.

As the yacht's captain navigated the vessel into the open water, Kylie worked to restore the flirtatious mood between them. Despite her best efforts, however, she couldn't replace the sad, bleak look in Drew's eyes.

AFTER THEY'D ANCHORED and the crew remained discreetly hidden, Kylie and Drew stripped down and dove into the dark Pacific. The air was warm and humid, the water felt refreshing. Despite his earlier blow-up—or maybe because of it—Drew had every intention of making this experience better than her wildest fantasy.

He handed her a glow stick. "So you don't get lost," he said, grinning.

He pulled her against him and kissed her. She tasted like saltwater and wine, a perfectly intoxicating combination. Her naked legs wrapped around his hips, and for a few moments the pumping movement of his legs suspended them both in the water. But his energy could be put to much better use. He guided them to the boat's ladder where he could hold on as they floated.

As she held on to him, he lowered his own glow stick between her legs and rubbed the side of it gently against her clit.

She squirmed and laughed. "Is that what I think it is?"

"I hope you're not opposed to creative uses for safety lights."

Her eyes fluttered shut as he continued to stroke her. "Mmm. I...think...I'm fine with whatever you just said."

She slid one hand down his back and around his waist to his hard cock. When her fingers wrapped around him and began stroking, he gave a little gasp of pleasure. "I'm going to forget how the fantasy goes if you keep doing that," he said in a tight voice.

He slid the glow stick inside her, teasing her with it gently, then moved it back over her clit in a rhythmic motion. "Oh," she gasped. "That's...okay. I...can't remember it, either."

He watched pleasure play across her features in

the moonlight. Having her this relaxed, this into the moment and him, almost erased the hollowness and fear that her relationship history had left him with. This was the Kylie he was fighting for.

"Mmm."

"You are the most beautiful woman I've ever seen," he murmured.

She opened her eyes and looked at him with a mixture of disbelief and gratitude.

"You are," he insisted. "Inside and out."

"You're too much."

"I meant inside as in, your personality, not your… but that's beautiful, too," he said, and she burst out laughing.

"Oh, this is so romantic," she said when she recovered. "I never imagined being seduced with a glow stick."

"Hey, it was working for a few minutes, wasn't it?" He hadn't intended laughter to be part of his get-busy-in-the-water scheme, but it seemed to be working if the intimate look in her eye was to judge.

"Yes," she said. "This is wonderful." But she couldn't contain her laughter.

It only got worse when he put the glow stick between his teeth and wiggled his eyebrows at her. "Sexy, no?" he said around the tube of glowing green plastic.

"Wildly."

"Am I ruining your whole fantasy?"

She stopped laughing and pulled him close, her fingers clasped around his shoulders. "Not at all. It's like you said, the reality blows the fantasy all to hell. I never could have dreamed this up."

She took the glow stick from his mouth and kissed him long and deep, while Drew cupped her ass with one hand and guided her to his erection. With little effort, he slid into her hot pussy, and the delicious sensation of it caused him to gasp against her mouth.

She moaned softly as he thrust deeper into her. He held the railing to the ladder as he found a rhythm, and she clung tightly to him, rubbing her clit against his body as they moved together.

He could feel her growing hotter and wetter around him, could feel her inner muscles tensing as she built toward a fast climax. It would be one of many for her tonight, if he had his way. He'd chartered the boat for the whole night, and he intended to make it around to the other side of the island in time for sunrise.

But right now, he lost all thought of past and future as his own body edged near climax. He heard himself gasping as his cock strained inside of her, then she came. Her body quaked against his, her insides growing even tighter and wetter, sending him over the edge on the heels of her orgasm. He spilled into her in great spasms, his body stimulated further by the ocean.

After a few moments, their climaxes passed, and he kissed her again, this time more gently. Now he was feeling the strain in his arms. She noticed his muscles quaking.

"Let's get back in the boat before we get eaten by a shark," she said.

And he watched her glorious backside as she pulled herself up onto the ladder. If he hadn't been so spent, the sight would have made him instantly hard. He followed, and they went to a blanket he'd spread out on the deck and lay down on it, then gazed up at the stars.

"Thank you," he said into the silence after a few minutes.

"*What?* No, thank *you*. It was incredibly sweet of you to put together this whole night for us, based on my silly little fantasy."

"My pleasure. But I do thank you for giving us this time together. It's been one of the best times of my life."

He hadn't meant to go all sentimental on her after his earlier outburst, but the stars, the night, the setting…there was no way around a bit of heartfelt sentiment.

But her relationship history and her continued reticence about any commitment to him held him back from what he most wanted to say—that he could have spent his whole life happily making Kylie's fantasies come true.

16

"I TOTALLY beat your time!" Kylie insisted the next day as the cool air of the hotel lobby enveloped her. The spacious area was crowded with people checking in and guests chatting or reading in numerous chairs and sofas scattered about. In her sweat-soaked workout gear she felt a bit underdressed and disheveled.

Drew, walking beside her, shook his head. "You did not. I was an eighth of a second ahead of you, at least."

"Liar!" she said and swatted him on the shoulder.

They'd just completed a sprint from the beach, and Kylie had been thoroughly impressed with herself for staying neck and neck with Drew the entire way. She wasn't about to admit defeat. So what if he'd been a little tired from diving all morning—she had to have something to give her an edge against his stamina.

He caught her against his chest and held her with her arms pinned at her sides. "If you don't admit I won, I'm going to tickle you until you pee on yourself, right here in front of all these genteel hotel guests."

"It'll probably embarrass you more than it'll embarrass me. People will just wonder why you're harassing that poor incontinent girl."

"That's it, you asked for it," Drew said and dug his fingers into her rib cage.

Kylie squealed. She'd never been able to tough out being tickled. And she'd made the mistake of confessing to Drew recently how easily it made her wet her pants.

A few people in the lounge area cast disapproving glances at them.

"Okay, okay," she said, gasping. "I give up!"

"You admit I won?"

"Yes…"

He stopped the tickling and loosened his grip on her enough that she could turn to face him. "Yes?"

She was going to tease him some more, but the happiness in his eyes struck her. The bleakness from last night had vanished and the result left her almost breathless. She wrapped her arms around his neck and kissed him.

He pulled her against him, and the kiss got a little more passionate than perhaps was appropriate for a public place. Kylie moaned softly at his tongue coaxing hers. Reluctantly she pulled away before anyone could tell them to get a room.

They already had a room, after all. They might as well go use it.

Before turning away, she placed one more light kiss on his lips as a promise of more to come as soon as they could get a little privacy. "Let's go get naked," she whispered.

As they headed toward the elevator, hand in hand, Kylie caught sight of a familiar face waiting in the check-in line. She stopped in her tracks.

She was screwed.

And not in any way she wanted to be screwed.

The entire passionate exchange with Drew had been witnessed by one of their superiors.

And not just any superior. Admiral Dunmead, the commander of the entire Naval unit she and Drew were assigned to was staring at them, a frown on his face. He looked different in his civilian clothes, but there was no doubting his identity.

Drew followed her line of vision. "Damn, isn't that—"

"The admiral."

"Oh, shit," he said under his breath.

"We'd better go say hello," Kylie said weakly, her heart sinking to her knees.

She should have known better. She *had* known better, but had chosen to ignore her own good sense. Hawaii was a frequent destination for military stationed in San Diego, for work and leisure. And many personnel stayed at this hotel that catered to the military. It was only a matter of time until they ran into a coworker. And they had—the worst possible coworker.

Releasing Drew's hand, she marched across the lobby with him at her side. She supposed there was a small chance the admiral wouldn't recognize Drew, given his lower rank and infrequent associations with the admiral. But Dunmead knew her.

She forced a calm expression on her face. If ever there was a time to invoke the ice queen, this was it. "Admiral Dunmead. It's so good to see you, sir." She extended her hand, and he shook it in his typical vise grip.

"Lieutenant Commander Thomas," he said evenly. "What a surprise." His gaze swept her head to toe and never had Kylie wished for the protection of her uniform more.

"And Ensign MacLeod, as well," he said to Drew, shaking his hand in turn.

"Hello, sir. What brings you to Hawaii? Business or pleasure?"

"Business. But apparently you two are here for pleasure." The admiral's tone made it absolutely clear that he did not approve.

"We're, um—" Kylie cleared her throat "—on mandatory leave. After the shooting."

"Right. I remember discussing it with Commander Mulvany."

"You were right. Getting off base was necessary. We—" What was she doing bringing Dunmead's attention to the fact she was here with Drew? "That is, I have appreciated the leave," she said, feeling like an idiot as she babbled on. "It's been a healing time."

"Lieutenant Commander, I'd like to speak with you privately when I'm done here."

Kylie nodded, her mouth going dry and her stomach twisting into a knot. "Yes, sir. Should I wait here in the lobby for you?"

"That's fine."

With a nod, he dismissed them both. Kylie cast a worried look at Drew as they walked away. He sighed and shrugged.

"I guess I'll wait for you in the room," he said as they neared the lounge area.

She could only nod, her mind reeling with dread.

After he left, she sat alone, waiting to hear her death sentence. This was her worst career nightmare come true—behaving inappropriately in front of her superior officer. She never should have agreed to this vacation. She should have stayed in San Diego, stayed on the job and dealt with her crap. She could have proven her worthiness as a Naval officer by persevering under pressure. She could have shown Commander Mulvaney that the little fainting episode was an anomaly and that she had control of herself.

Instead she'd let a moment of weakness dictate her actions. She'd jumped Drew at the first chance and continued to make one bad decision after another.

And she'd gotten so caught up in her lust for Drew that she'd let it happen, when it could have been prevented.

Damn it. Damn it. Damn it.

She wanted to kick herself.

What would she say to the admiral? Would she try to excuse herself? Plead temporary insanity? She hated the idea of making excuses.

No. She would face the music. She'd been wrong, she'd acted inappropriately and she deserved whatever punishment she got.

Agonizing minutes later, Admiral Dunmead finished checking in and approached. Kylie straightened.

"Lieutenant Commander, I assume you are aware that fraternizing with direct subordinates is conduct unbecoming an officer."

Hearing the words spoken aloud was a shock to her system. "Yes, sir," she said quietly.

"I confess, I'm surprised by your behavior. You

have an exemplary service record and this is the last thing I would have expected from you."

Under his sharp regard, Kylie's insides shriveled. Once again she'd disappointed, she'd failed someone in authority whom she'd sought to impress. The weight of it threatened to buckle her.

"However, I'm aware you've been operating under mental duress lately. Because of that and your record, I'm prepared to offer leniency. I will report your behavior to your commander and let him decide what your punishment will be. Understood?"

She more than understood. She'd been granted a temporary reprieve that she did not entirely deserve. She could still face severe consequences, but not right now. "Yes, sir. Thank you, sir."

"And I don't want to see you fraternizing with that ensign—or any other—again, do you hear?"

"Yes, sir," Kylie said, barely able to meet his gaze.

The admiral, finished with her, turned on his heels and marched away, leaving Kylie to seethe in her own shame.

Her parents had been right all those years ago. She had awful judgment, and she should never be left to her own devices. She was an incompetent fool. Worse, her superiors knew it, too.

Kicking herself every way she knew how, she went upstairs to end her fling with Drew.

KYLIE WATCHED the people on the dance floor, her own body still soaked in sweat. She and Drew had danced until her feet, clad in strappy high-heeled sandals, couldn't take any more, and now they were sitting at the bar having a drink.

She'd spent the afternoon since talking to Admiral Dunmead feeling miserable, knowing she'd have to leave Hawaii and all the comfort she'd found there with Drew. He'd been so concerned for her that she hadn't had the heart to tell him they were over. Cowardly, she knew, but her low spirits had needed the care that only Drew gave her. Tomorrow, she promised herself. She'd tell him tomorrow. For tonight she'd absorb every last drop of enjoyment she could. It wasn't likely the admiral would be here at this club, so she could have some fun.

Except, she didn't seem able to escape her thoughts. They cycled through her demolished career to breaking the news they were over to Drew. She wasn't sure she'd even be able to say those words aloud.

She was so very grateful to him for helping her heal. The thought of hurting him now tortured her.

And he would be hurt. She'd sensed he had a lot invested in this fling, although she'd managed to skirt most attempts to discuss what was between them. Still, he'd done nothing to deserve it.

Forcing the gloomy thoughts away, she sipped her beer and elbowed Drew. "I had no idea you had such rhythm," she teased.

"I don't like to reveal all my tricks in one shot."

"You certainly don't need a strategy for how to impress the girls."

He pulled her close. "There's only one girl I'm interested in impressing, and I've got my hand on her thigh right now."

Kylie looked down at his hand creeping up under the

hem of her dress. "Be careful what you start," she warned.

He smiled mischievously. "Be careful what you promise."

She felt a slight warmness in her cheeks. With little provocation she knew he'd drag her into the nearest bathroom to have his way with her.

Next to them, a drunken man raised his voice at someone else, then stumbled sideways into Kylie.

When he didn't apologize, Drew put his hand on the man's arm and held him firmly. "Watch it, man."

"Oh, sorry," the guy slurred, then turned his attention back to the guy he'd been talking to.

"Pretty rowdy crowd in here tonight," Kylie said, glancing around the busy bar.

On the stage across the room, a cover band played dance music, and the enthusiastic group on the dance floor had spilled into the rest of the bar, creating a wild energy in the place.

"You want to get a little fresh air?" Drew asked, and Kylie gratefully nodded.

She followed him through the crowd to the lobby, where they got their hands stamped and ducked outside into the sultry evening air. It wasn't that much cooler, but the relative quiet and lack of people were a relief to her senses.

No sooner had they escaped the noise, though, than a buzzing sound came from Drew's pocket. He pulled out his cell phone and looked at the display.

"It's the friend who's watching my cat. I'd better answer," he said, then flipped open the phone and said, "Hey, man, what's up?"

Kylie started to turn her attention elsewhere to give him some privacy, but she couldn't help listening in a little bit.

"It's awesome. I'm having the time of my life."

He was?

"Yeah, hey, it's good to hear from you, but I'm kind of in the middle of something... No, I'm here alone... How's Lola?"

Lola? Was that his cat?

"Is she eating her prescription food okay?"

Definitely the cat. Kylie tried not to smile at his choice of names as she walked ahead of him. The breeze did a wonderful job of cooling her skin. She was wearing a little green sundress with spaghetti straps that crisscrossed her back multiple times, and a pair of gold heels that were going to be the death of her feet if she didn't get out of them soon.

Drew joined her. "That was my friend Justin. You remember him from the bar, right?"

"Yeah, sure. I've seen him around the base, too."

"I have a feeling he suspects something's up. Ever since that night he's been pumping me for information about you. He's convinced something happened between us and doesn't believe I came on this trip alone."

"Technically, you did, since we were on different flights. Guess it's impossible to avoid speculation."

"You know, he mentioned a story about Seaman Caldwell's arraignment being on the news today. I haven't watched any news since the shooting happened."

"I only did once, and I immediately regretted it." Seeing the horrific events she'd experienced firsthand reduced to a sensational headline and a few talking points had emphasized the tragedy. She'd been so angry at the way the media treated their lives—hers and the victims' and the families'—that she'd wanted to throw her TV at the announcer. Perhaps the day would come when she could again view news coverage without the urge to do bodily harm.

"So," she said, eager to change the subject. "I was eavesdropping on you. Are you really having a great time?"

Drew closed the distance between them. "I really am," he said and took her into his arms to kiss her. "Can't you tell?"

"Um, yeah," she said. "I can tell."

Kylie closed her eyes and felt a wave of happiness mixed with regret wash through her. When Drew pulled away, she took a deep breath and looked up at the starry sky.

"Beautiful night," she said, trying not to sound sad.

"Beautiful girl," Drew murmured, watching her. "It's nice to see you looking carefree."

Thank God he'd misinterpreted her expression. He hadn't been as worried by Admiral Dunmead's admonishment as Kylie was. Drew thought that the admiral deferring her reprimand to her commander was a sign of how lenient the Navy would be with her so there wasn't any real reason to let the episode ruin their vacation.

If only Kylie could be so genuinely carefree.

He took her hand in his and led her along the walkway toward the beach. They passed other couples taking advantage of the romantic setting, and soon they came to the edge of the beach and an empty bench.

"Let's sit," he said. "Rest your feet."

She sat and he tugged her feet into his lap. When he took off her shoes and began massaging her left foot, she moaned gratefully.

"Oh God, that feels good. Thank you."

"My pleasure."

She smiled. "Is this the part where I discover you're really a robot lover and not an actual human guy?"

"If I were a robot lover, I'd be a terrible swimmer, I'm pretty sure."

"Good point. Nonetheless, sometimes you seem too good to be true."

He looked at her seriously then. "You seem so much more happy and relaxed than you did in San Diego."

"Yeah, I guess this trip accomplished what it was supposed to, huh?"

"For both of us."

"I'm in the best shape of my life," Kylie said. "Both mentally and physically."

"Mentally, too? Really?"

She nodded. "I think so."

"That's great. I was afraid you'd let the admiral get to you too much."

She shrugged. She was about to clarify that her improved mental state had taken a serious hit from the admiral, but she didn't want to ruin Drew's vacation, too. "No, it's okay. I agree with you—there's no use worrying about the consequences now."

"Good. The rest of the world can wait for us."

"Yeah. I'm not letting it dominate my every thought," she said, then realized she'd gone too far and had started sounding as though she was trying to convince herself of her own words.

Drew cast an odd look at her, but said nothing.

"I've loved being here with you…" Her voice trailed off again. God, now she was sounding as though she was saying goodbye.

Why couldn't this go on forever? She'd been avoiding thinking about how it would feel to leave Drew. It was going to hurt like hell, no way around it.

She didn't want to go back to San Diego.

Since that night on the yacht and Drew's outburst she'd felt a shift in her feelings for Drew. His comments about her past and behavior toward him had opened her eyes to how much more she wanted from… from herself. That shift terrified her. She was getting too attached.

"Hey," Drew said, catching her mood change. "It's going to be okay, you know. We'll have each other to get through the repercussions, just like we do now. Whatever happens, I'll stand by you in whatever way you need me to."

She couldn't look at him so faced the ocean. Moonlight reflected on the waves, and she tried to keep all emotion from her face. They wouldn't have each other. And she was too lacking in courage to admit to him that she couldn't continue their relationship. She needed to steer this conversation in safer directions.

"I still feel like I can never trust the universe the way I used to. Like any minute now, it could all fall apart." The shooting was much safer.

"That's one of the hardest things about life, that there aren't any guarantees. But that doesn't mean we can't relax and enjoy ourselves as best we can."

"I guess," she said.

"I haven't had any nightmares in two weeks," Drew said.

"You know, whenever I went to bed I'd feel the weight of those deaths on my chest. I couldn't sleep. The weight was unbearable. Soon as I got to Hawaii, the weight went away."

"Maybe none of it will come back."

"Whatever happens, this trip has been good for me. More than I can even say. Thanks for inviting me."

She didn't want to veer into smarmy territory, but he deserved to know that she hadn't completely sacrificed this time for her career.

"I'm glad it's helped you." He smiled then. "And I'm hoping this foot massage has helped enough to keep you dancing with me a little longer tonight."

"My feet feel about a million times better. Thank you."

She slipped on her shoes and let him lead her back toward the nightclub. As they neared, the music and din of people got louder. Once inside, they had to squeeze close together to maneuver through the crowd.

They found their way to the edge of the dance floor, and they were about to start dancing when several people started yelling nearby. Angry voices rose above the music. Drew looked over to see what was going on, and people began to scramble out of the way.

A fight had broken out near the bar. Two men, one

of them the drunken one who'd bumped into Kylie earlier, were pushing each other and hurling insults, while onlookers seemed more interested in watching than intervening.

Kylie looked around for a bouncer, but there wasn't one in sight. Then she saw that several men were distracting the bouncer at the front entrance. They must be friends with the brawling men. She muttered a curse.

Someone screamed, and when she glanced around, she saw that one guy had drawn a gun and was pointing it at the drunken man. She felt a cold bolt of terror shoot through her.

Not this.

Not again.

She grabbed Drew's arm.

"Get out of here!" he yelled, pushing her toward the door. "Go for cover."

But she couldn't leave him behind. She couldn't live with herself if anything happened to him. In her mind she saw Campbell shooting at her coworker, turning the gun on Drew, on herself...

No.

Courage would not abandon her again. She knew what to do.

Chaos had erupted, and the man fired a warning shot. It hit the floor. The drunk hurled himself toward the shooter, trying to grab the gun. They fell to the ground, grappling and throwing punches.

Kylie saw the gun slide free and, without thinking, she dove for it. Drew, seeing what she was doing, threw himself at the men and pinned them while she got her hands on the weapon.

A moment later, she had it firmly in her grasp, and Drew was holding one of the men while the bouncer, who'd finally gotten into the room, restrained the other.

She felt tears welling. It was over. In a matter of seconds, her life had flashed before her eyes, along with Drew's, along with everyone else's that she'd seen die in her office that day.

But this time it was different. She watched as the two men were dragged out of the bar, and four police officers entered and took over. One of them relieved her of the gun, another started asking her questions. She answered as best as she could, concentrating to keep the two incidents separate in her mind.

She kept looking around for Drew, wanting reassurance over and over that he was safe. And he was.

He was safe.

Later, after the scene had calmed down and the police had finished taking reports, after she and Drew had walked home in stunned silence, there weren't any words.

Kylie only knew that she felt a relief like no other she'd experienced. A relief like rain after a long draught. She felt as if something about their fates had changed, that they'd gone from being the ones who had no control to being the ones who could turn the tide.

She'd trained to defend, and this time she hadn't let her training down. She might never again have complete confidence in her ability to perform in a crisis, but she'd proven that she could, when called upon, react appropriately in an emergency.

She could save someone after all.

She never questioned or considered resisting what started happening once they were back in her hotel room. Drew stripped off her clothes, then his own. He turned on a lamp beside the bed, and he covered his body with hers as they lay down together.

He kissed her with overwhelming emotion. Maybe it was her imagination, but she didn't think so.

He ran his hands up and down her torso, over her breasts and her neck and her face and her hair, down her hips and over her thighs and calves. He cupped her bottom in his hands and pulled her to his mouth, plunging his tongue into her, teasing her most sensitive spots. He did it all hungrily, as if he'd never been with her before, as if he was proving to himself that he could really have her.

Kylie grasped at the sheets and gasped at the delicious sensations between her legs as he licked her. As she neared climax, her every coherent thought vanished. She rocked her hips in time with his tongue. When he finally plunged his fingers into her, she climaxed, crying out at the blinding pleasure.

Her inner muscles contracting, she writhed against him until the orgasm passed. She pulled him up to her, kissing him as he entered her, then burying her face in his shoulder so he wouldn't see the tears in her eyes.

She didn't want this to end, but there was no place for them to go. And if she stuck around any longer, she'd never be able to leave.

17

KYLIE AWOKE to the familiar feel of a warm body next to hers. Before she could snuggle into Drew again she got the horrible sinking feeling that she had to leave. Now. In the middle of the night. Like a coward.

But if she lingered until morning, she wasn't sure she'd have the courage to go. She couldn't face him right now and explain that she didn't have the balls or whatever it took to pursue a relationship, given their circumstances. Let him think the worst about her— that she'd again chosen her career over a man, that she'd never been fully engaged with him. Whatever it took for him to forget her.

Not that she'd be forgetting him anytime soon.

She muttered a silent curse that she was again buckling to external pressure. The carefree woman she'd been in Drew's company couldn't withstand the scrutiny of Admiral Dunmead and the Navy. One harsh glance from a senior officer and she was once again a new recruit desperate for approval.

However wonderful she felt in Drew's arms, she still felt ashamed. Around him, she was, quite simply, a reckless fool. She was supposed to be the more mature one of the two of them, the one with more wisdom, experience and self-control. She had none of those qualities. She wasn't brave enough to defy the Navy and embrace a possible future with Drew. So, by default, the Navy won—they got to keep her.

When she looked at his sleeping face, so perfectly handsome and kind, the air of strength and courage that surrounded him all the time apparent even now, she knew he deserved better. He deserved to live his life with someone who would put him first. She had too much baggage to be capable of that sacrifice so she needed to leave him before she did something really stupid, like fall in love.

Like fall in love.

Oh dear God. The moment she let the words cross her mind, she knew it had already happened. That feeling that had struck her their first night together… she'd hung around long enough for it to take root and grow.

She'd provided it with sunshine and nutrients and water, and it had blossomed into something that couldn't live.

Her heart thudded double time. There was no doubt. She was in love with Drew, and she had no one but herself to blame for the pain their breakup would cause.

Outside the window, the sun was cresting the horizon, casting a slight glow on the morning sky. With no idea where she would go or what she would do, Kylie eased herself out of the bed, quietly dressed and gathered her belongings into her bag. She cast frequent nervous glances at Drew, but he slept on in oblivion.

When she was ready to go, she paused at the door,

and her stomach bucked at the idea of walking out this way. Drew would never abandon her without saying goodbye. But she couldn't face the anger or disappointment in his eyes, or hear his arguments for why she should stay.

There wasn't anything for her to say in her defense. She had to salvage her career because she knew who she was serving—her country. Anything else was too big for her to handle. He might not be happy with her decision, but he would understand.

But she couldn't go without even leaving a note. She glanced at the desk across the room, with its hotel stationery and pen. Then she crept silently over to it and began writing.

> I'm sorry I can't stay anymore. I hope you can understand. Good luck. You'll make a great S.E.A.L.

Ugh. It was lame, and awful, but better than nothing. She folded it in half, tiptoed to her pillow and placed the note on it.

Then she went back to the door and eased it open silently. Blinking away the dampness in her eyes she stepped into the empty hallway alone.

"DAMN IT! Answer your phone, Kylie. I'm going to keep calling until you do!"

Drew hung up his cell phone, threw it on the bed and muttered another curse, this one to himself. He'd dialed Kylie six times today, but each time he'd only gotten her voice mail. Ever since he'd woken to find her missing from the hotel room with nothing but a vague, pointless note left behind, he'd been angry, shocked and bewildered.

But the longer he went without talking to her on the phone, the more he was forced to face the fact that she'd simply done what she'd been itching to do from the start—run away from him. History repeated itself. That didn't make the reality sting any less.

He paced across the room outside to the balcony. Suddenly Hawaii seemed like a dreary place, in spite of the beautiful scenery and sunshine. Having her disappear out of the blue, just when he'd been sure they'd really connected, made him itch to blow out of paradise.

Damn it, Kylie. Damn it, damn it, damn it.

He should have known. She'd never wanted a relationship with him. She'd made that clear from the start.

Well, sort of clear. She'd wanted him for sex, but she hadn't wanted the accompanying emotions.

He should have known a thirty-four-year-old woman who'd never been in love before was a woman to be avoided with a twenty-foot pole.

Spotting the note she'd left that morning, he crumpled it in his hand, then threw it into the garbage. He had so much pent-up rage, he hardly knew what to do with himself. He'd channeled as much of it as he could into working out earlier, but still he seethed. He wasn't going to feel any relief until he talked to Kylie.

He grabbed the phone from the bed. This time, he dialed her home phone rather than her cell. She had to be back home by now, and if he was lucky, she wouldn't have caller ID.

After four rings, she answered.

"How dare you leave me here with nothing but a note," he said by way of greeting.

Silence on the other end of the line.

He hadn't considered how best to keep her on the phone.

"If you hang up on me, I won't stop calling. You have to talk to me sooner or later. You owe me that."

She sighed. "You're right. I'm sorry."

"How do you think it felt to wake up and find you gone?" he said, his voice thick with emotion.

"I—I couldn't face you. I knew you'd talk me out of leaving. And I had to leave."

"No, you didn't. You just did what was most convenient for you and your goddamn career."

"That's not fair."

"Isn't it? You used me to distract yourself, and when you were done, you wanted out as easily as possible."

She didn't respond.

Maybe he'd touched a nerve. Rather than backing off, he said, "So much for your flawless character. Turns out you're just as big a coward as you feared you were, huh?"

He knew he was hitting her where it hurt most now, and he had no intention of letting up—until he heard her crying.

Almost immediately, his anger drained, and he fell silent as he listened to her sob and sniffle. Cruel as it was, it felt good to know she was in pain, too. He didn't want to believe she could simply walk away from him and feel nothing.

But finally, she spoke, her voice remarkably free of emotion. "I am very sorry I've hurt you. I understand your need to lash out right now, but please know I want the best for you, and that is why I left."

She sounded like Lieutenant Commander Thomas again, not the woman he'd known as his lover. Calm, cold and stiff, he pictured her in her freshly starched uniform, her hair restrained in a bun.

"Oh, really? Your actions were totally selfless?" Sarcasm oozed from his tone.

"Of course not. No one's are. But I did consider you in making my decision. I'm not the right woman for you, Drew. You and I both know that."

"Don't tell me what I know. You don't get to order me around in my personal life the way you do at work."

"You're right, but much as you may not want to admit it," she said coolly, "the Navy dictates a lot about our personal lives. You know it's part of the reason we can't be together."

Drew bit his lip. He wanted to yell at her, to rail and rage and throw the phone out the window, but he felt as if he wasn't even talking to the same woman he'd fallen for. This other Kylie he barely recognized. She was the straitlaced boss he hadn't even given a second thought.

He imagined her more passionate side being held hostage inside her stiff facade, and his anger dissipated. If this is how she had to be to survive, if she was too afraid or fragile to be the vibrant, passionate woman he cared about, then truly, all he could do was feel sorry for her. Because this other version of her…it was no way to live.

Was she going to spend her whole life trying to be perfect—or this warped version of it—in order to get other people's approval?

If so, then yeah, she'd done him a favor by walking away.

"I feel sorry for you," he said, then hung up the phone.

18

DREW'S WORDS ECHOED in Kylie's head all night. She'd tried her best to forget their final conversation, but she'd never had anyone slap her in the face with a statement of pity before.

She deserved his anger, but not his pity. Anything but that.

She tried to tell herself he was lashing out in the cruelest way he could, but something about the tone of his voice suggested he hadn't spoken in anger at all. He'd been sincere, she feared.

Kylie parked her car in her assigned spot at the office. It was 8:00 a.m. and her stomach twisted tighter and tighter as she turned her thoughts from Drew to her task at hand. She had to face Commander Mulvany and admit her wrongdoing. She wasn't sure if he'd spoken to the admiral yet, but it didn't matter one way or the other.

The honorable thing to do was to confess the whole story herself and face the consequences. She walked slowly toward Mulvany's office, the morning air still heavy with coastal fog. For a moment, she wished she was still in Hawaii.

But no.

She was here, in her own life where she belonged, not there, living out a fantasy. All was as it was supposed to be. And she deserved to feel as awful as she did.

Inside the building, Commander Mulvany's secretary wasn't at work yet. Her desk sat empty, and the door behind it stood open with the light on. Kylie stepped into the doorway and knocked gently to get the commander's attention.

"Lieutenant Commander, come in," he said, distracted.

She stepped into the room and took a seat across from him.

"Welcome back from vacation," he said as he put down the document he'd been reading and gave her his full attention.

"Thank you, sir."

"Did you get plenty of rest?"

"Yes, sir."

"That's great. You're looking a lot better than the last time I saw you."

"I'm feeling better, too. You were right, I needed the break."

"You've still got more time off, don't you? Are you ready to return to work?"

Kylie hesitated. Was she? She didn't know what to say to that, so she decided to cut to the chase. "Actually, sir, I came here to speak to you about a different matter."

"Yes?"

He must not have known, or else he'd have brought it up by now, wouldn't he? Maybe he was waiting for her to do the right thing and confess.

"I accompanied one of my subordinates to Hawaii, sir—Ensign MacLeod."

"Right, he was one of the survivors of the shooting, I recall. Quite the hero that day," Mulvany said solemnly.

"Yes, well, MacLeod and I developed an inappropriate romantic relationship after the shooting. I've ended the relationship, but I am ashamed of my behavior nonetheless."

Her commander cocked an eyebrow at her. "Why are you confessing this to me now?"

"I—I'd like to say it's purely out of my own sense of honor and duty, but I'm sorry to say Admiral Dunmead saw MacLeod and I together in Hawaii. I wanted to let you know, in case he hasn't talked to you yet, so that you wouldn't be taken by surprise."

"I talked to the admiral yesterday, but he didn't mention seeing you."

Kylie wasn't sure whether to feel relieved or bewildered by that. "I suppose he's got much more important matters to think about than my personal life."

"As we all do. I suggest you keep this matter private and move forward, behaving with the utmost professionalism from this point on."

"Yes, sir, but…" She paused, confused by his lack of a reaction. "I'm not sure if I can continue to work with Ensign MacLeod in the same way I have in the past."

"Are you saying a reassignment is necessary?"

"No," she said, surprised at how sure she sounded even though she'd never considered this option. "Actually, I'm not. MacLeod is due for a promotion, and he's about to take the S.E.A.L. test, so he won't be working under my command for much longer."

"Then what's the issue?"

"What I should have said is, I'm not sure I'm cut out to serve anymore at all."

His expression lit up with surprise. "What leads you to this conclusion?"

Good question. She was as surprised as he was to hear herself saying it aloud.

"My time in Hawaii gave me a chance to reflect. And of course, my relationship with Ensign MacLeod has brought into question my moral fitness as an officer—"

"You used poor judgment, but given the set of circumstances—the trauma you two have been through— there's not a jury that would judge you as harshly as you seem to be judging yourself."

"But—" Kylie felt the absurd urge to defend her belief that she'd behaved reprehensibly.

"There's no question your actions were inappropriate, but unless the admiral cares to make an issue of it—"

"No, sir. He said he intended to leave the matter to you to handle."

"Good. I'm inclined to move forward as if none of this happened. If, however, I hear the slightest word of your consorting with your subordinates again, there will be serious repercussions."

"I'm afraid, sir, my heart isn't in service to the Navy anymore." She was making it up as she went along, but it was true.

"Are you saying you want to leave the Navy?"

Leave the Navy. The phrase washed over her like a

breath of fresh air. She exhaled all the tension in her body and nodded.

"Is this because of the shooting? Because of your relationship with MacLeod?"

"No, sir. Well…yes and no. It's because of everything. I think recent events have only forced me to face a realization I've been coming to for a while. I'm ready to move on to the next phase of my life, and the Navy isn't a part of it."

He nodded solemnly. "I'm sorry to hear that. I don't suppose I should try to talk you out of it?"

"No, please don't. My mind is made up."

"Okay, well, let me know what I can do to help you in the transition to civilian life."

"I will, sir. And thank you for being so understanding of my recent actions."

She stood to leave, and they said their goodbyes. When she was alone again, she felt tears sting her eyes. Tears of relief, she realized. She'd owned up to her bad behavior, and this time, she'd been forgiven.

She'd been forgiven. It had seemed too easy, but Commander Mulvany had hardly blinked at her confession.

Kylie swiped at her damp cheeks and laughed at herself. She was amazed that she hadn't seen before what she needed to do. She was leaving the Navy, and the decision made the weight of her entire adult life lift from her shoulders.

The world was wide-open for her to explore anew. And one thing was for sure—she was done being her parents' daughter, living by their rules and consequences. She was ready to be fully her own woman.

Maybe she'd never get their forgiveness, but that was okay.

It was time to forgive herself.

19

Six weeks later...

KYLIE'S ENTIRE BODY ached from the cold water and the long workout, but she couldn't stop smiling. She'd just caught one of the best waves of her life, and Sonya had been on the beach videotaping the whole thing.

Until today, she hadn't been surfing since Hawaii. She'd nearly sold her surfboard a few years ago, it had collected so much dust, but now she was glad she hadn't. The time in Hawaii had reminded her how much she loved the sport. And when she had officially retired from the Navy, she was going to surf as much as she wanted.

She hauled her board to where Sonya sat on a blanket, then dropped onto the sand next to her friend.

"That was awesome," Sonya said. "I got the whole thing."

"Excellent."

Kylie stretched her back and shoulder muscles as they watched the crashing surf.

"So you're really going to do it, huh?" Sonya asked.

"Retire, you mean?"

"Yeah, it's just, I can hardly imagine you not being a Navy officer."

"You won't have to imagine, because you'll be face-to-face with the reality in another week."

"So, seriously. You spend a couple of weeks on a tropical island and you're ready to toss your whole career and start over?"

Sonya knew Kylie too well. She fixed Kylie with a stare as if her patience for allowing Kylie to share the sordid details in her own time had just expired.

Kylie usually told her friend everything, but this time, she felt afraid to divulge the whole truth. Partly because she wasn't sure she wanted to admit it to herself, and partly because she wasn't sure she understood everything that was happening to her.

"C'mon. What's really going on?" Sonya prodded.

"I wish I could explain it clearly…" When she trailed off, Sonya sighed.

"Does this have something to do with that twenty-something guy you've been suspiciously vague about?"

Kylie felt her cheeks redden. She knew in a flash that she was afraid of how her friends and family would react to the idea of her investing deep feelings in Drew.

"It does, doesn't it?"

Kylie glanced at her friend, then looked back down at the sand and nodded. "Yeah, I haven't told you everything that happened with him."

"Gee, let me guess. You go off to Hawaii with a hot young guy and you…um, let's see, *fall* for him, perhaps?"

"Is it that obvious?"

"Kylie, don't be stupid. You haven't gotten any action since the Dark Ages. Of course it's that obvious.

Besides, you came back glowing like you'd gotten thoroughly laid."

"I did?"

"Yep." Sonya leaned back on her elbows, sunning her belly. "So spill. I want all the dirty details."

There wasn't any point in hiding the truth now. So Kylie launched into the complete story of how she fell for Drew and how she'd crept out of the hotel room like a coward. Her friend nodded and murmured encouraging sounds as she listened, and by the time Kylie reached the point where she'd decided she couldn't live her life for the Navy anymore, Sonya was looking at her as if seeing her for the first time.

"Wow," she said when Kylie went silent. "You've really seen the light."

"I guess so. I mean, when I went to my boss to confess what had happened with Drew, I opened my mouth and out came my decision to leave the Navy."

"Good for you."

"And yeah, there's nothing like losing your big chance at love to make a girl wake up and smell the retirement papers."

"But how do you know he wouldn't give you another chance?"

Kylie felt a bit of tension drain from her shoulders. "So you don't think my relationship with him was horribly inappropriate?"

"Why would I?"

"Because he's eight years younger than me? And he's my subordinate?"

Sonya shrugged. "I've always thought those military rules you follow are crazy, and age ain't nothing but a number, babe. If you meet a guy and you dig him and he digs you, why get caught up in worrying that he grew up listening to the Backstreet Boys while you listened to George Michael?"

Kylie rolled her eyes at her friend's simplification of the issue. "You know it's more than just that. It's about maturity, and life experience and—"

"And you being afraid to go for it?"

"No!"

"Let's look at the situation. You're a smart, attractive, thirty-four-year-old woman who hasn't gotten laid in at least a couple of years. You haven't even had the prospect of a relationship—not even a *date,* for God's sake."

"I've been busy!"

"Even the leader of the free world manages to have a personal life, while you—"

"The leader of the free world doesn't have to deal with sexism, far as I know. I felt like I needed to focus totally on my career at the time, but now I've seen the error of my ways, okay?"

"I'm only trying to keep it real. You can't tell me you haven't been afraid of getting involved with a guy."

Kylie felt like arguing further, but really, what was the point? To protect her silly pride? "Okay, fine. I've been a total chicken shit. Are you happy now?"

"Absolutely." Sonya's expression was vaguely triumphant, but her eyes twinkled with mischief. "I just wanted to hear you say it."

She was joking, but Kylie realized by the sudden lightness in her chest that saying it really did count for something. Better yet, accepting it was true…it mattered. She really had been afraid.

She thought of the safe feeling that came with making all the safest choices, with walking the narrowest path possible, following a course someone else's good intentions had laid out for her. It all amounted to an imminently safe—and utterly boring—life.

"You know," Sonya said, her tone softer now, "you're not a teenager anymore. You can bend or break the rules without your whole world coming to an end."

Kylie could hardly think of her teenage years without seeing expressions of pain and disapproval on her parents' faces. It was ridiculous. She was too old to be letting a mistake she'd made at the age of seventeen affect her life so much.

"I know," she said. "You're right."

"So what are you going to do about it? Let true love pass you by?"

Kylie sighed. She hadn't heard a word from Drew since that last horrible phone conversation, when he'd told her he felt sorry for her. He hadn't called, and she mostly felt relieved by that.

Mostly.

She knew he'd passed the S.E.A.L. test, but he wasn't due to arrive in San Diego until tomorrow. And of course she was keenly aware of his impending arrival, in spite of her repeated insistence to herself that she had moved on.

She had received an invitation to his promotion ceremony. He'd been waiting to pin on his new rank for months, thanks to the limits of government money dedicated to promotion raises, and finally the ceremony was scheduled for next week. He'd probably only invited her out of formal obligation since she was his boss for now, but…it would still be appropriate for her to attend the ceremony.

"No, I'm going to give it a try," she said quietly, not quite sure what that meant.

Sonya leaned over and gave her a squeeze around the shoulders. "That's my girl," she said.

And suddenly, Kylie knew what she had to do.

20

DREW STOOD STRAIGHT and tall as the new rank of lieutenant, junior grade, was pinned to his collar. His expression carefully blank, he looked out at the crowd of his friends and coworkers. This should have been one of the happiest moments of his adult life—his first promotion as a Naval officer—second only to learning last week that he'd made the S.E.A.L. team. But something was missing.

He'd scanned the crowd at the start of the ceremony, and the one person he'd hoped against hope to see among the faces had not been there. He should have known she wouldn't come. And he'd told himself she wouldn't. But now, he realized by the heavy weight of disappointment in his chest, his promotion meant very little to him without her there to celebrate it.

Then, a strawberry-blond head in the last row caught his eye, and he saw her. She must have slipped in partway through without his noticing. His chest swelled with relief and other emotions he didn't want to consider now, and he blinked away a sudden dampness in his eyes.

Kylie was here, after all.

It was his turn to talk now, to address those who'd gathered to celebrate this moment with him. He'd had a speech planned out in his head, and he took the written version of it from his pocket as he stood at the lectern, but his entire being was focused on her. There was no way he could stand here and read the dry speech he'd prepared last night.

Instead he spoke freely into the microphone and the words flowed out of him.

"Ladies and gentlemen," he began. "Thank you for joining me to celebrate this momentous day of my career." As he spoke, his gaze never left Kylie. "As I stand here, I see among you people whom I owe gratitude for all of my growth and achievement as an officer. I see colleagues and mentors who've selflessly passed along their wisdom, and I am deeply indebted. I could not have grown as a person or as an officer without your guidance. You are the very embodiment of heroism. In your quiet, everyday acts of courage, you exemplify what it means to be an officer of honor and integrity."

As he wrapped up the speech with a few closing words, he caught the welling of emotion in Kylie's eyes. She understood he was talking about her. She may not have believed those words about herself, but it meant the world to him that she knew he believed them.

No matter what happened between them personally, she was a hero in her own right, and she deserved to know it.

When the ceremony ended, he had no choice but linger and talk to those who wished him well. He only wanted to talk to one person. His gaze sought her out repeatedly as he accepted congratulations and listened to small talk. She was frequently watching him, too.

It was the first time he'd seen her since returning from Hawaii. She looked more relaxed now. Her tan hadn't faded, but the tension around her eyes had.

When he finally made his way over to her, she smiled warmly and hugged him.

"Congratulations," she said. "You've got a great career ahead of you."

He didn't want to hear more small talk—not from her. "It's good to see you," he said, the huskiness in his voice revealing more depth of emotion than he'd intended.

"Good to see you, too," she said seriously. "I was hoping we could talk privately after this."

"How about right now?"

"But your guests—"

Around them, caterers had set up tables of food in the outdoor pavilion. Appetizers and drinks were being served, along with a cake that Drew would be expected to cut soon. He didn't give a damn, though. Not now.

"They won't even notice I'm gone."

She looked doubtful, but she said, "Maybe we could walk out to the beach?"

He nodded, and they headed away from the hotel garden where the ceremony had been held, toward the sounds of seagulls and crashing surf.

What could she want to talk about? He didn't dare to hope. She'd already made her feelings clear. She probably wanted to give him some sage career advice, pass on whatever wisdom she'd gained as an officer.

Which would be nice, he supposed, but the very thought of it was a punch in his gut. Wisdom wasn't what he wanted from her.

They reached the sand, and Kylie slipped off her heels to carry them. Drew tried not to notice how she looked, but she was too gorgeous to ignore. She wore a white sundress that revealed a hint of cleavage, her hair upswept so that her neck and shoulders were exposed. The light dusting of freckles on her shoulders made him want to reach out and touch her. He knew how soft and warm her skin would be, just as well as he knew how she'd smell like sweet citrus…

No, he had to stop that kind of thinking right now.

No more, he told himself. Not another thought.

They reached the waterline where the sand was cool and damp from the waves. Kylie stopped walking and turned to face him, her expression serious but otherwise inscrutable.

"I wasn't fair to you," she said.

"Wasn't fair to me how?" His chest tightened, afraid of what she might or might not say.

She looked up at him, her big green eyes brimming with emotion. Her soft pink lips turned up at the corners, forming the slightest of smiles. "I shouldn't have held your age against you. You're clearly old enough to know what you feel and what you want, and I denied that. I'm sorry."

"Thank you," he said stiffly, wishing that wasn't all she had to say.

But then she spoke again. "I realized something else."

"What?" he asked, his voice barely audible above the sounds of the waves.

"I've fallen in love with you."

He blinked, the news striking him momentarily dumb. Even he hadn't dared to hope she'd say *that*.

"You have?"

"Yes." She was watching him carefully, probably anxious for his reaction. "I've done a lot of soul-searching since I came back from Hawaii, but that was one thing I didn't have to do much searching to figure out."

She smiled tentatively then, and he could see that she needed desperately to hear his response. But he was afraid to believe the answer to his happiness could be this simple. There had to be a catch, a problem—something. Questions swirled in his head.

"But what about your career? And what about caring what everyone else thinks?"

"None of it matters," she said, sounding both vehement and frustrated. "I *love* you!"

"I love you, too," he said, unable to pretend it wasn't true.

Then he took her in his arms and bent his head to kiss her. She felt better than he remembered, her lips eager but pliant. She kissed him with enough enthusiasm that he couldn't doubt she was happy to be in his arms again.

When they broke the kiss, she said, "I don't want to be apart from you again."

"If you'll marry me, you won't have to be."

Her eyes widened in shock at his words. Then she smiled again. "Are you serious?"

He hadn't planned on saying it, but he'd been speaking from his heart, he knew. He'd known from their first night together that there was something incredibly special about them together, and it hadn't taken him much longer to know she was the woman he wanted to spend his life with.

"Dead serious," he said. "Will you marry me?"

She wiped a tear from her cheek and nodded. "Yes," she said. "I will."

Drew felt like doing a cartwheel right there on the beach, or letting out a victory yell, or... The idea of them never being apart again might sound nice, but given his new assignment as a S.E.A.L., and Kylie's steady rise in the ranks of the traditional Navy, they were going to spend months—even years—of their lives apart.

His heart sank.

As if she sensed his sudden change of mood, she said, "I decided to take early retirement."

Drew stared at her, stunned and uncomprehending. "But... You're a great officer. I thought you loved your career."

She shook her head. "I used to love the challenge of it. But it was always what my parents wanted for me. It wasn't until we were in Hawaii together that I started realizing what I want for myself."

"What is that?"

"I want a life, not just a job. I want a family someday, and a partner, and time to spend with my partner. If I stayed in the Navy on the track I'm on, I'd never have any of that."

"But some people manage it," he argued weakly, not really wanting to change her mind, but feeling obligated not to take her away from something she loved.

"True, but I know in my heart that I couldn't, and I don't want to do the important stuff halfway."

"What do you want to do, then?"

"Training with you in Hawaii reminded me of how much I love diving. For now, I'm taking a job as a diving instructor here in San Diego. And I'm going to get back into taking pictures, maybe specialize in underwater photography. See if I can get a freelance gig going with it. When you move to your next duty station, then I'll figure out what to do there."

"Wow," Drew said, stunned.

This really could work. They'd still have the inevitable separations of the military, but they wouldn't be compounded by dual careers with dual deployments.

"You'll really get early retirement?"

She nodded. "The Navy has more officers of my rank than it needs right now, so they're happy to get rid of me."

He took her hand, and they walked toward the hotel garden and the promotion party.

"What made you change your mind?" he asked, his wounded pride finally having a chance to smart now that he felt secure that he was getting what he wanted so badly.

"I didn't really have to change my mind. I always knew I wanted you, from the first time I ever laid eyes on you. But I did have to allow myself to face the truth. In some ways you're more mature than I am, and I had no business thinking age had much to do with it."

He grinned. "Age does have something to do with it."

"Oh?"

"I'm old enough to recognize a hot old chick when I see one."

She slapped his shoulder in mock outrage. "Don't push your luck, buddy. I may be old, but I'm stronger than I look."

He caught her hands in his and pulled her against him. "Don't ever doubt for a second that I think you're the hottest woman I've ever laid eyes on."

Her eyebrows shot up suspiciously. "Hottest for an old chick?"

"Just plain hottest."

"I don't think I believe you."

"Wait until after this party and I'll show you exactly how I feel." He pressed his pelvis against her abdomen so that she could feel his stiff cock.

Her gaze turned mischievous. "What if I can't wait?"

"Then we'll have to bow out early."

"Like right now?"

"Sounds pretty reasonable to me," Drew said, suddenly changing direction to head for the parking lot.

With Kylie at his side, nothing was out of the question.

* * * * *

Turn the page for a sneak preview of
AFTERSHOCK, *a new anthology*
featuring New York Times *bestselling author*
Sharon Sala.

Available October 2008.

n●cturne™

Dramatic and sensual tales of paranormal romance.

Chapter 1

October
New York City

Nicole Masters was sitting cross-legged on her sofa while a cold autumn rain peppered the windows of her fourth-floor apartment. She was poking at the ice cream in her bowl and trying not to be in a mood.

Six weeks ago, a simple trip to her neighborhood pharmacy had turned into a nightmare. She'd walked into the middle of a robbery. She never even saw the man who shot her in the head and left her for dead. She'd survived, but some of her senses had not. She was dealing with short-term memory loss and a tendency to stagger. Even though she'd been told the problems were most likely temporary, she waged a daily battle with depression.

Her parents had been killed in a car wreck when she was twenty-one. And except for a few friends—and most recently her boyfriend, Dominic Tucci, who lived in the apartment right above hers, she was alone. Her doctor kept reminding her that she should be grateful to be alive, and on one level she knew he was right. But he wasn't living in her shoes.

If she'd been anywhere else but at that pharmacy when the robbery happened, she wouldn't have died twice on the way to the hospital. Instead of being grateful that she'd survived, she couldn't stop thinking of what she'd lost.

But that wasn't the end of her troubles. On top of everything else, something strange was happening inside her head. She'd begun to hear odd things: sounds, not voices—at least, she didn't think it was voices. It was more like the distant noise of rapids—a rush of wind and water inside her head that, when it came, blocked out everything around her. It didn't happen often, but when it did, it was frightening, and it was driving her crazy.

The blank moments, which is what she called them, even had a rhythm. First there came that sound, then a cold sweat, then panic with no reason. Part of her feared it was the beginning of an emotional breakdown. And part of her feared it wasn't—that it was going to turn out to be a permanent souvenir of her resurrection.

Frustrated with herself and the situation as it stood, she upped the sound on the TV remote. But instead of *Wheel of Fortune,* an announcer broke in with a special bulletin.

"This just in. Police are on the scene of a kidnapping that occurred only hours ago at The Dakota. Molly Dane, the six-year-old daughter of one of Hollywood's blockbuster stars, Lyla Dane, was taken by force from the family apartment. At this time they have yet to receive a ransom demand. The housekeeper was seriously injured during the abduction, and is, at the present time, in surgery. Police are hoping to be able to talk to her once she regains consciousness. In the meantime, we are going now to a press conference with Lyla Dane."

Horrified, Nicole stilled as the cameras went live to where the actress was speaking before a bank of microphones. The shock and terror in Lyla Dane's voice were physically painful to watch. But even though Nicole kept upping the volume, the sound continued to fade.

Just when she was beginning to think something was wrong with her set, the broadcast suddenly switched from the Dane press conference to what appeared to be footage of the kidnapping, beginning with footage from inside the apartment.

When the front door suddenly flew back against the wall and four men rushed in, Nicole gasped. Horrified, she quickly realized that this must have been caught on a security camera inside the Dane apartment.

As Nicole continued to watch, a small Asian woman, who she guessed was the maid, rushed forward in an effort to keep them out. When one of the men hit her in the face with his gun, Nicole moaned. The violence was too reminiscent of what she'd lived through. Sick to her stomach, she fisted her hands against her belly, wishing it was over, but unable to tear her gaze away.

When the maid dropped to the carpet, the same man followed with a vicious kick to the little woman's midsection that lifted her off the floor.

"Oh, my God," Nicole said. When blood began to pool beneath the maid's head, she started to cry.

As the tape played on, the four men split up in different directions. The camera caught one running down a long marble hallway, then disappearing into a room. Moments later he reappeared, carrying a little girl, who Nicole assumed was Molly Dane. The child was wearing a pair of red pants and a white turtleneck sweater, and her hair was partially blocking her abductor's face as he carried her down the hall. She was kicking and screaming in his arms, and when he slapped her, it elicited an agonized scream that brought the other three running. Nicole watched in horror as one of them ran up and put his hand over Molly's face. Seconds later, she went limp.

One moment they were in the foyer, then they were gone.

Nicole jumped to her feet, then staggered drunkenly. The bowl of ice cream she'd absentmindedly placed in her lap shattered at her feet, splattering glass and melting ice cream everywhere.

The picture on the screen abruptly switched from the kidnapping to what Nicole assumed was a rerun of Lyla Dane's plea for her daughter's safe return, but she was numb.

Before she could think what to do next, the doorbell rang. Startled by the unexpected sound, she shakily swiped at the tears and took a step forward. She didn't feel the glass shards piercing her feet until she took the second step. At that point, sharp pains shot through her foot. She gasped, then looked down in confusion. Her legs looked as if she'd been running through mud, and she was standing in broken glass and ice cream, while a thin ribbon of blood seeped out from beneath her toes.

"Oh, no," Nicole mumbled, then stifled a second moan of pain.

The doorbell rang again. She shivered, then clutched her head in confusion.

"Just a minute!" she yelled, then tried to sidestep the rest of the debris as she hobbled to the door.

When she looked through the peephole in the door, she didn't know whether to be relieved or regretful.

It was Dominic, and as usual, she was a mess.

Nicole smiled a little self-consciously as she opened the door to let him in. "I just don't know what's happening to me. I think I'm losing my mind."

"Hey, don't talk about my woman like that."

Nicole rode the surge of delight his words brought. "So I'm still your woman?"

Dominic lowered his head.

Their lips met.

The kiss proceeded.

Slowly.

Thoroughly.

* * * * *

nocturne™

NEW YORK TIMES BESTSELLING AUTHOR

SHARON SALA

JANIS REAMES HUDSON
DEBRA COWAN

———

AFTERSHOCK

Three women are brought to the brink of death...
only to discover the aftershock of their trauma has
left them with unexpected and unwelcome gifts of
paranormal powers. Now each woman must learn to
accept her newfound abilities while fighting for life,
love and second chances....

Available October wherever books are sold.

Silhouette

SPECIAL EDITION™

FROM *NEW YORK TIMES* BESTSELLING AUTHOR

LINDA LAEL MILLER

A STONE CREEK CHRISTMAS

Veterinarian Olivia O'Ballivan finds the animals in Stone Creek playing Cupid between her and Tanner Quinn. Even Tanner's daughter, Sophie, is eager to play matchmaker. With everyone conspiring against them and the holiday season fast approaching, Tanner and Olivia may just get everything they want for Christmas after all!

Available December 2008
wherever books are sold.

SILHOUETTE

SPECIAL EDITION™

BRAVO FAMILY TIES

Tanner Bravo and Crystal Cerise had it bad
for each other, though they couldn't be more
different. Tanner was the type to settle down;
free-spirited Crystal wouldn't hear of it.
Now that Crystal was pregnant, would
Tanner have his way after all?

Look for

HAVING
TANNER BRAVO'S
BABY

by *USA TODAY* bestselling author
CHRISTINE RIMMER

Available in October wherever books are sold.

REQUEST YOUR FREE BOOKS!

2 FREE NOVELS PLUS 2 FREE GIFTS!

HARLEQUIN®

Blaze™

Red-hot reads!

YES! Please send me 2 FREE Harlequin® Blaze™ novels and my 2 FREE gifts (gifts are worth about $10). After receiving them, if I don't wish to receive any more books, I can return the shipping statement marked "cancel". If I don't cancel, I will receive 6 brand-new novels every month and be billed just $4.24 per book in the U.S. or $4.71 per book in Canada, plus 25¢ shipping and handling per book and applicable taxes, if any*. That's a savings of 15% or more off the cover price! I understand that accepting the 2 free books and gifts places me under no obligation to buy anything. I can always return a shipment and cancel at any time. Even if I never buy another book, the two free books and gifts are mine to keep forever.

151 HDN ERVA   351 HDN ERUX

Name	(PLEASE PRINT)	
Address		Apt. #
City	State/Prov.	Zip/Postal Code

Signature (if under 18, a parent or guardian must sign)

Mail to the **Harlequin Reader Service**:
IN U.S.A.: P.O. Box 1867, Buffalo, NY 14240-1867
IN CANADA: P.O. Box 609, Fort Erie, Ontario L2A 5X3

Not valid to current subscribers of Harlequin Blaze books.

Want to try two free books from another line?
Call 1-800-873-8635 or visit www.morefreebooks.com.

* Terms and prices subject to change without notice. N.Y. residents add applicable sales tax. Canadian residents will be charged applicable provincial taxes and GST. Offer not valid in Quebec. This offer is limited to one order per household. All orders subject to approval. Credit or debit balances in a customer's account(s) may be offset by any other outstanding balance owed by or to the customer. Please allow 4 to 6 weeks for delivery. Offer available while quantities last.

Your Privacy: Harlequin Books is committed to protecting your privacy. Our Privacy Policy is available online at www.eHarlequin.com or upon request from the Reader Service. From time to time we make our lists of customers available to reputable third parties who may have a product or service of interest to you. If you would prefer we not share your name and address, please check here. ☐

HB08R

Inside ROMANCE

Stay up-to-date on all your romance reading news!

The Inside Romance newsletter is a FREE quarterly newsletter highlighting our upcoming series releases and promotions!

Click on the <u>Inside Romance</u> link on the front page of **www.eHarlequin.com** or e-mail us at insideromance@harlequin.ca to sign up to receive your FREE newsletter today!

You can also subscribe by writing us at: HARLEQUIN BOOKS Attention: Customer Service Department P.O. Box 9057, Buffalo, NY 14269-9057

Please allow 4-6 weeks for delivery of the first issue by mail.

IRNBPA208

HARLEQUIN®

COMING NEXT MONTH

#423 LETHAL EXPOSURE Lori Wilde
Perfect Anatomy, Bk. 3
Wanting to expand her sexual IQ, Julie DeMarco selects Sebastian Black—
hotshot PR exec—to participate in a no-strings fling. The playboy should be
an easygoing love-'em-and-leave-'em type, but what if there's more to the man
than just his good looks?

#424 MS. MATCH Jo Leigh
The Wrong Bed
Oops! It's the wrong sister! Paul Bennet agrees to take plain Jane
Gwen Christopher on a charity date only to score points with her gorgeous
sister. So what is he thinking when he wakes up beside Gwen the very next
morning?

#425 AMOROUS LIAISONS Sarah Mayberry
Lust in Translation
Max Laurent thought he was over his attraction to Maddy Green. But when
she shows up on the doorstep of his Paris flat, it turns out the lust never went
away. He's determined to stay silent so as not to ruin their friendship—until
the night she seduces him, that is.

#426 GOOD TO THE LAST BITE Crystal Green
Vampire Edward Marburn has only one goal left—to take vengeance on
Gisele, the female vamp who'd stolen his humanity. Before long, Edward has
Gisele right where he wants her. And he learns that the joys of sexual revenge
can last an eternity....

#427 HER SECRET TREASURE Cindi Myers
Adam Carroway never thought he'd agree to work with Sandra Newman. Hit
the sheets with her...absolutely. But work together? Still, his expedition
needs the publicity her TV show will bring. Besides, what could be sexier than
working out their differences in bed?

#428 WATCH AND LEARN Stephanie Bond
Sex for Beginners, Bk. 1
When recently divorced Gemma Jacobs receives a letter she'd written to
herself ten years ago in college, she never guesses the contents will inspire
her to take charge of her sexuality, to unleash her forbidden exhibitionist
tendencies...and to seduce her totally hot, voyeuristic new neighbor....